The Ballad of

GATO GUERRERO

Also by Manuel Ramos

The Ballad of
GATO GUERRERO

Manuel Ramos

With a foreword by Alfredo Véa Jr.
and an introduction by Ilan Stavans

LATINO
VOICES

Northwestern University Press
Evanston, Illinois

Northwestern University Press
Evanston, Illinois 60208-4210

Northwestern University Press edition published 2004. Copyright © 1994 by
Manuel Ramos. Foreword copyright © 2004 by Alfredo Véa Jr. Introduction
copyright © 2004 by Ilan Stavans. First published 1994 by St. Martin's Press.
All rights reserved.

Printed in the United States of America

10 9 8 7 6 5 4 3 2 1

ISBN 0-8101-2091-7

Design by Basha Zapatka

Library of Congress Cataloging-in-Publication data are available from the
Library of Congress.

The paper used in this publication meets the minimum requirements of the
American National Standard for Information Sciences—Permanence of Paper
for Printed Library Materials, ANSI Z39.48-1992.

For Mom and Dad.

Thank you, Mercedes.

I always expected
That you would see me through
I never believed in much
But I believed in you.
"From Hank to Hendrix"
—*Neil Young*

◆

El día que yo me muera
No voy a llevarme nada
Hay que darle gusto al gusto
La vida pronto se acaba
Lo que pasó en este mundo
No más el recuerdo queda
Ya muerto voy a llevarme
No más un puño de tierra.
"Un Puño de Tierra"
—*Carlos Coral (D.A.R.)*

Contents

◆

Foreword

◆

Alfredo Véa Jr.

I had just received a copy of *The Ballad of Gato Guerrero* for my birthday and decided to read it during a flight down to Mexico. I had already read Manuel Ramos's first novel, *The Ballad of Rocky Ruiz,* and was looking forward with great delight to his second offering. As it happened, I slept all the way down to Guadalajara. I didn't even read the EXIT signs.

My friend in Guadalajara is a rabbi, and I soon found myself in the back of his lovely synagogue with another rabbi and an Irish Catholic priest. There we were, a lawyer, two rabbis, and an Irish priest. In any town in America or Ireland this would have been the beginning of a joke.

An hour later I was looking for any means of escape. I was desperate. I had bombed completely. Every Jewish or Irish joke that I told those three men died right there on the table. Each one of those men sat there like an oil painting. Each one was wondering who the hell I was and what I was talking about. Then I realized what had happened. Those

Sephardic Jews and that Irishman had never been steeped in the American East Coast.

They had not been shoved together with Africans and Italians into a fomenting cauldron that would forge tap dance, vaudeville, jazz, and burlesque. In Mexico their contribution would be substantial, I'm sure, but it would never be a culture of loquacity and humor. Mexico has many things that I love, but it has no shtick, and the great distance from their homeland has left the Irish (to my eyes) far too sober, too pacifistic—and, worst of all, too taciturn.

On my way back home I began to ponder the question of Mexican and Latino artists in Aztlán and elsewhere in the United States. How would Chicano artistry fare in places like Denver and Chicago? Had there been a cultural transformation as with the rabbis in Mexico? Had that transformation been a positive or negative one?

I found myself completely *verklempt* and *fishmayed*. In order to clear my head I ordered a double whiskey, neat, and then another. To keep from becoming totally obsessed with the question, I opened *The Ballad of Gato Guerrero* and was immediately amazed and soon . . . overjoyed. All of my *nachas* was gone.

There they were, intact yet transformed: all of the ancient and honored forms of the genre that flow directly from Poe, Conan Doyle, Hammett, and Chandler. There on every page was that nagging internal dialogue, that philosophical insurrection, that dark counterweight to many of our cherished myths of the American dream and of a staid and polite society.

There, mixed with the spice and ambience of Chicano *cultura* and history, were the flawed and precarious people who daily wound one another, and the marred people who pursue them, unravel with blemished reasoning their defective crimes, and bring them to imperfect justice. Every mystery writer is a not-so-secret anarchist, reminding us darkly that entropy is the power that will win out when all is said and done. Yet the writer is mortally persistent in insisting that smatterings of order and logic count for something. It's the best that Luis Montez can do, and he does it well.

The rabbis and the priest in Mexico have probably never seen a trench coat or felt a chill so cold that the only warm thing in their universe is a fifty-dollar bill in their pants pocket. I doubt that any of them has ever seen a woman walk into their offices—a blond with legs that go from here all the way to there. But the next time I'm down in Guadalajara, I'll make it a point to tell them that a Chicano up in Denver has embraced a traditional genre and transformed it into a separate and distinct voice and has done it with virtuosity. Manuel Ramos has grabbed the baton and is running with it. The transformation is more than positive. Once in a while, that's the way things happen up here in El Norte.

Since that flight to Mexico I have had the great pleasure of meeting Manuel and his lovely wife, Flo, in Denver. Against Flo's advice Manuel positively luxuriated in giving me a guided tour of the seediest Chicano bars in town. I could see that he didn't really belong in those places with those people. But I could also see that without his presence entropy would soon swallow them all. His protagonist belongs, and so do all of his characters.

As he moved between the tables and chairs, Manuel seemed to sense that he was there to give a tiny piece of redemption, a minuscule slice of immutability, to all of the *vatos* and homeboys, to their chaos. That's what good writers do.

So now . . . *entonces,* when I've had enough of Sam Spade, and Cecil Younger is giving me *shpilkes,* I can turn to Luis Montez. *Gracias,* Manuel!

Introduction

◆

Ilan Stavans

Crime, sex, and ideology . . .

Edgar Allan Poe, the writer responsible for the essay "Eureka," the poem "The Raven," and the story "The Murders in the Rue Morgue," is credited as, among other things, the inaugurator of the mystery genre on the American landscape. But Poe, a nineteenth-century itinerant drunkard and newspaper reporter incapable of holding on to a steady job, infuriated one too many editors and remained in an eternal stage of transition—from Baltimore to New York, from lucidity to madness. Superficially, at least, Poe was an anarchist. Or was he?

Manuel Ramos is a confessed descendant of Poe: orangutans are always to be found in the closet. But Ramos isn't an anarchist. He may be impatient with authority, but

This is the second of a four-part reconsideration of Manuel Ramos's novels with Luis Montez as protagonist. The other three parts appear as introductions to, chronologically, *The Ballad of Rocky Ruiz, The Last Client of Luis Montez,* and *Blues for the Buffalo,* all reissued by Northwestern University Press in the series Latino Voices.

he understands that, for Chicanos to be respected, it isn't enough to subvert power: it is also important to share it.

After all, Ramos is a veteran of the culture wars. His Luis Montez sagas aren't about forensic science but about community: the anger and complacency of, in his own words, "these the people I know so well." He adds: "Whatever they are dealing with, it's going to come up in my books. Life's political and all I can do is hope that I'm at least being fair." His work is also about promiscuity.

So to Poe's desire to solve a crime by giving supreme authority to reason (the French love him for that), in his oeuvre Ramos adds the two other components of the triptych: sex and ideology. He does it using his own experience as a source of wisdom. "I've never found a body in my office, nor have I ever solved a murder," he claims, "but I've had some clients who wanted to kill me."

I have a personal letter from Ramos dated November 22, 1994. It accompanied a copy of *The Ballad of Rocky Ruiz.* Its reception, the year prior, had been positive, and the second Montez installment, *The Ballad of Gato Guerrero,* was already out. "I'm keeping my fingers crossed," he wrote to me. But he was cautious: the industry of mystery novels moves too fast from one fashion to the next, hardly giving an author enough time to breathe. And multiculturalism—how long would it last as a trend? Would Ramos and other "ethnics" be mercilessly pushed aside by an apathetic audience known for its loyalty but also for its impatience?

That Montez volume is a meditation on friendship and liaisons between fathers and sons. Poking fun at the pop cartoon *Felix the Cat,* it delves into domestic and police brutality. The detective is going against an "almost continual antagonism he faces as a Latino in a white world." Deciphering a case is rewarding, but Ramos, clearly, is after an altogether different target: the mysteries of the Chicano self.

But Ramos faced criticism: Was the second Luis Montez novel too similar to the first? The worst criticism came from inside the Chicano community. Were *Rocky Ruiz* and *Gato Guerrero* airing dirty linen? This type of critique was to be expected. Indeed, the ethnics are often celebrated outside, by the nonethnics, as heralds bringing important news to the world at large. The pals in the neighborhood, instead, accuse them of *no ser suficientemente chicano*—in Ramos's situation, of "distorting the truth so that Anglos get a better handle on us."

As a Jewish *mexicano* whose journey to El Norte came in his midtwenties, I know firsthand about attacks such as these. I've been accused by professional Chicanos of being an interloper, a foreigner looking in. But is Ramos one, too— another Tío Tomás? Impossible: he's as much an insider as one can get—an advocate for the poor who, by the way, regularly teaches a course on Chicano letters at Denver's Metropolitan State College.

Happily, Ramos was unfazed. His third Montez case, *The Last Client of Luis Montez,* would be proof of it. Rather than doctoring an upbeat life, the detective descends to the circles of Dante's Inferno. He gets divorced and is beaten, ridiculed by his own peers, caught in a bullet rainstorm, and even crippled. But as the fine *superhéroe* he parodies himself to be, Montez bounces back again and again. No circumstance is too decisive to finally break him apart. He's a Chicano *hecho y derecho,* lonely and nostalgic, perhaps, but a man of *orgullo*—pride.

A critique of *chicanismo* from inside out is offered—and I admire this Montez installment for its bravery. Through its pages, the reader is able to understand the dilemma at the heart of *la chicanidad:* To be or *no ser*? The answer is ideological, and ideology is messy. How to be part of a group penalized for not assimilating in full? What are the clues to unravel in order to cope with the half-baked nature of Mexican American life, the so-called in-betweenness of being part here and *en parte de allá*?

The response is a mystery trapped in a solution.

---◆---

After years of scraping by, I suddenly found myself to be an involved, culturally aware person—Mr. Cool and Clean—a man on the brink of business success, at least in terms of paying my bills. If it hadn't been for Felix Guerrero, I might have plodded quietly through my American dream. But Felix was a friend, and if friends don't occasionally shake things up—hey, what good are they? The price for such friendship probably is cheap in the long run. What's a little death in return for a minute or two of love?

Ah, Gato. You had a way, man. You had a way . . .

1

I squinted at a stage of flashing lights: red, blue, yellow, green, red, blue, yellow, green. A pattern of clichéd southwestern icons framed the musicians. Garish howling coyotes, thunderbirds, and desert lizards vibrated with each loud note. Rhythmic guitar riffs echoed through the park, a drum set a polka cadence, and a skinny, bent-over old man, pumping and squeezing a beat-up accordion with every ounce of soul left in his shriveled body, sang about confronting the pain from the lost love of his beautiful brown lady by drinking all the tequila in south Texas.

Couples bobbed in a fast-moving counterclockwise circle. Dark-eyed women in jeans or flowery skirts swished their hips as their men twirled them in and out, forward and backward. The grace and affection of people releasing themselves to the music dizzied my brain and warmed my heart.

Teenagers, *viejitas*, lawyers, trash collectors, low-riders, ranchers, Chicanos, Pueblo Indians, whites and blacks— the last night of the festival had brought together every race and class. A syncopated sea of Stetsons, glistening boots, and shiny jewelry moved with the music. Sweat

1

mixed with beer and sloppy kisses on the dance floor. I could have reached out and touched the lust.

Those not dancing watched with expert eyes, nodding their heads at those who understood the need to be precise in their routines, praising the new steps of old friends, laughing at the strangers who had no idea what they were doing. They sat at picnic tables or on their own lawn chairs, consumed platefuls of spicy enchiladas, greasy fried potatoes, and roasted corn with chile powder, and compared this year's music with every other festival.

The accordionist smiled, mystified by the love all these lucky people had for the music he had learned from his father and grandfathers, music that had been played for decades, ignored except by the fans who gathered for wedding dances on Saturday nights, Sunday-afternoon *parrandas* at recreation centers and Knights of Columbus halls, or the occasional *matanza*.

Felix and Elizabeth were in the middle of the crowd. They had sailed by a couple of times, two-stepping like pros, laughing and hugging each other, as lovers should. I searched for Felix's bright blue shirt with the purple, orange, and brown embroidered Indian symbols across the back, or for Elizabeth's billowy western skirt flaring around her red cowboy boots. Bumping into them on the dance floor seemed the only way for me to connect. For that, I needed a partner.

Ah, the women of New Mexico! In every size and color, I was surrounded by Chicana beauty—*flaquitas, gorditas, güeritas, prietitas.*

The music stopped to applause and whistles. A florid, almost hoarse announcer with shoulder-length hair and a red bandanna looped around his forehead rushed to the stage and eagerly shouted to the throng.

"Ay-ay-ay! *¡Qué bonita música!* Another hand for the grand master—Epifiano Morales. He can still pump it out, eh? And we're only getting warmed up! Next is a real special treat! Somebody none of you want to miss. The man we've been waiting for all night! All the way from Alice, Texas! Number one in *tejano* music today—Tony C.! Yes, Tony Candelaria . . . *¡y su conjunto!*"

A piercing female scream sliced through my eardrums. Groups of tittering girls flocked around the stage. Obviously, the past year had been good for Candelaria—big sales, awards, number-one songs, and now the final act at the Española Music Festival. Tony Candelaria had arrived in the big time.

Ernesto López stood next to me, a beer can in his hand and a wide grin plastered across his dark, sunburned skin. We had met at Evangelo's in Santa Fe only a few hours before when I waited for a message from Felix. He had a friendly face and a dry sense of humor—a *manito* who fit in easily with the bar's tourists and townies. He had casually started a conversation about the music festival, Chicano art and culture. We dealt only with important matters. Just how naïve was the promoter who hired a Texas band for a New Mexican fiesta? It had to be a good sign that *la música* was heard on the FM stations, no? Was it true that serious artists preferred living in Española over Santa Fe?

My swallow of beer dried into coal dust when I saw the gun tucked away in a shoulder holster underneath Ernesto's trim western-cut leather jacket. The events of the past few weeks had made me jumpy and for an instant I thought about walking away and leaving Ernesto at the bar with his drink and weapon. Is that any way to live? A metal detector at Evangelo's swinging door would have uncovered at least another dozen guns toted by men and women in the New Mexican cantina. Was I supposed to insulate myself from all human connection? When Felix finally called and said to meet him at the dance around ten, I had offered Ernesto a ride in my rented car.

The band's crew took twenty minutes to set up the

equipment. Four burly, ponytailed men, crammed into Tony Candelaria T-shirts, plugged in microphones, tested the sound level, and laid out the instruments within easy reach of the musicians.

Ernesto and I were at one end of the stage, close to the action, hemmed in by the buzzing fans who fingered cameras and eight-by-tens of Tony C., impatiently whistling and hollering for their man. I had to shout to talk with López.

"This guy is hot, eh? These girls look like they're ready to faint."

Ernesto's grin grew even wider. Turquoise and silver glittered from his fingers and wrists, and, I assumed, on the handle of his *cuete*.

"Tony C. has it made, man. Any *ruca* he wants, whenever he wants her. Making money like a hippie rock and roller. Texas ain't big enough for him anymore."

"How about Denver?"

"Sure, man. Sooner or later. With gambling in the mountains, there'll be more clubs, more bars. I myself left almost a thousand in *pinche* Central City just a few weeks ago. They can pay Tony C. out of that!"

He chugged his beer and looked around for the nearest MEN sign.

The crowd surged forward, stuffing us into the barricades surrounding the stage.

Tony C. nonchalantly strolled onto the stage and picked up his accordion. He was as pretty as his picture. Young and cocky, he sported a wide, floppy white sombrero with a two-inch handwoven band, tight, crisply creased jeans, an orange shirt, and a yellow neck scarf.

The roadies finished their work and climbed from the stage to the barricade, where they swaggered, arms folded across their chests. I understood why they resembled Latino versions of overweight professional wrestlers. I was trapped in a wall of flesh that wanted only to storm the stage and rip off Tony C.'s colorful and provocative clothes. I considered asking the guards whether I could stand behind them, for my own protection.

And then the music started.

Tony C. tore into a classic *tejano* tune, and I would have sworn he ripped apart his specially designed diatonic accordion. He whirled his machine around his head and across his back, sweat already lubricating his face. His instrument gleamed in the stage lights and reflected its own colors—red, white, and green. Across the accordion's pleats, an angry eagle gripped a snake in its beak, expanding and shrinking with every move of Tony's hands. His bony fingers flew across the buttons in a sophisticated impersonation of Jimi Hendrix techniques. Tony's voice carried across the park and into the homes of grandmothers who sang along as they watched flickering TV sets and tapped their slippers on linoleum floors.

If I could have moved, I would have grabbed the first agreeable woman and we would have danced and hollered and sung and acted like coyotes screaming at the white moon, and no one would have noticed us, because they all would have been doing the same. I decided that this festival was all right.

I turned to give Ernesto the good news, but he was gone.

Laughing, Elizabeth and Felix rolled into me.

"Louie, Louie. 'Bout time you made it, bud. Get ready to see the best. Tony C. and his psychedelic squeeze box!"

My lanky friend held Elizabeth close to him, shielding her from the crush of the crowd. Her eyes gleamed. The flush that played on her skin betrayed that she was winded from dancing, catching her in intimate reflection of her passion for Felix.

I wanted to ask about details that should have been important. For starters: What did they think they were doing? Had they been careful? Did Trini know where they were? But Felix made a move for the dance floor just as I started to speak, and I knew it wouldn't do any good to talk to them. Common sense and rationality had been dumped in Colorado. They pushed through the throng, looking for a way to the jammed but less crowded dance floor.

The blue-green-and-silver streak to the immediate right of Felix dredged up the coal dust from Evangelo's and clogged my throat. I wondered how Ernesto had slipped away and reappeared so quickly. The scene struck me as odd immediately, but I couldn't put my finger on what bothered me. Maybe it was the stage lights reflected on the barrel of the gun in Ernesto's hand. I shouted Felix's name but was drowned out by the music. Dozens of fans cut me off from my friends.

Ernesto pointed the gun at Felix's back. I grabbed handfuls of clothing and tried to move people by throwing them out of my way.

"Hey, man!"

"What the . . ."

"¡Qué chinga, dude!"

The people shoved back. A chubby, round-faced Chicano in a cowboy hat with a rhinestone-studded golden crucifix hanging from his neck threw a punch at me. I ducked and he missed my nose by a fraction of an inch, but in that instant I lost Felix and Elizabeth. I desperately eyed the mob scene when the shots rang out. There were screams and thuds and even the band missed a beat.

A football exploded behind me. Over my shoulder, I saw Tony C. limp across the stage, blood flowing across the left side of his orange shirt, smeared into his beautiful accordion. Another band member rushed to help him, but Tony dropped to his knees.

Men and women ran in every direction, away from the wrestlers on the dance floor. Ernesto's jacket rolled around the concrete floor, amid the shapes and grunts of others in the fight. The heaviest of Tony C.'s guards jumped over the barricade and landed a few feet from the brawl. He grabbed the gun. The guard, older than his cohorts but obviously very quick, yanked the weapon from the assassin's hand and used it to knock him down. Ernesto flailed at Felix's savior, but the man was having no trouble. He held Ernesto by the neck, pinned to the ground.

In the chaos, the guard quickly surveyed the scene until his eyes fixed on me. He motioned with his head toward Felix and his unspoken message was for us to run while we still could.

Elizabeth and Felix looked at me.

"Let's go! Follow me to the car!"

We ran from the dance floor, past the food and beer vendors, and out through the gate. Cop cars squealed into the parking lot, sirens blaring, but we ignored them and raced off in the opposite direction. In a matter of minutes, we were hurling down the highway.

"That guy I met at the bar—one of Anglin's men! I led him right to you!"

Elizabeth squeezed my hand.

"Trini has contacts all over the Southwest. He must have known where we were as soon as we hit town. He had you followed from Denver. They would have found us sooner or later, Louie. We knew it had to happen."

A car pulled up beside us in the right-hand lane. I couldn't pass it. I slowed down, but it wouldn't pass me.

Felix peered into the night at the men in the car.

"Shit! It's that guy, the one who tried to blow my brains out. They've caught us, Louie!"

We sped across the New Mexican landscape in the general direction of old Mexico. At eighty miles an hour, I had a hard time avoiding the cars in my lane, but Ernesto kept with us.

Felix pushed Elizabeth down onto the seat.

"Watch out! They're going to shoot!"

7

I jerked the steering wheel and swerved the car. The bullet missed. Ernesto whipped his car to avoid me and he lost control in the gravel of the shoulder. I screeched into an exit at the last possible minute. We were in the arroyos and hills around Santa Cruz. I slammed the accelerator and turned off the headlights. Dirt, weeds, and rocks spewed out behind us.

I fought the steering wheel of the small red rental in a losing battle. I had given up control of the car five miles back, but my passengers didn't need that information right then. Felix gripped the dash with one pale hand and with the other he clung to Elizabeth like a drowning man reaching for a rope. She rolled and tumbled between us, sliding across the seat with each twist and turn of the vehicle I was allegedly driving.

The engine whine cut across the scrub country. I could feel the car falling apart underneath us. Cactus, piñón and squat mesquite bushes flowed alongside in a bad imitation of a Rio Grande flood. Our pursuers' headlights in the rearview mirror appeared much closer than they had only a few seconds before.

Felix hollered, "You've got to lose them! They're right on our ass!"

Elizabeth hugged him and buried her face in his shoulder.

I tried to sound calm, but it was a useless gesture.

"It's no good. This tin can is no match for their machine. We've got to—"

I felt a blast that seemed to take hours to build and finish. The rear window splintered. Cool mountain air and pieces of glass slammed into the back of my neck. Elizabeth screamed. The wheel wrenched free. In the instant before the car flipped and we sailed through the star-splattered sky, I saw her hands covered with blood. I tried to breathe, but all I could manage was watching the earth

8

float away beneath us as the car turned over and over, tumbling through air and darkness.

I raised my face from the dirt and shook my head to jar my eyes into focus. The hulk of the car—twisted and dead—lay smoking off to my right. At ground level, I couldn't see much. No Felix, no Elizabeth. Except for a hissing from the wrecked auto, I heard no other sounds. I lay on the ground for several minutes, testing my bones and muscles for breaks or tears. The blackness seemed to slip under my skin and flow with my blood.

I was about to sit up when a snap as loud as a freight train stopped me. A pair of dusty boots crept in my general direction. The moon cast a shadow across an arroyo. It looked like a giant in a cowboy hat, holding a gun, moving quietly and quickly. I silently asked myself the basic question: How had I let Felix talk me into this?

2

———————◆———————

Stale cigarette smoke clung to the pool players like clumps of musty *lana*. Ricocheting balls cracked sharply in the numbing din of jukebox music, the shouts and hollers of drunken men celebrating their talent on the shabby green surfaces, and the barely audible sighs of wasted time.

Felix Guerrero carefully watched his adversaries saunter around the pool table to the beat of fifties rhythm and blues. He snickered and groaned each time they shot, and Felix the Cat realized he hated pool, but there he was—and he had to be good. Eight ball: If you play, make it good or don't play at all.

The Fifth Annual Eight Ball Pool Classic had progressed through a dirty, dreary winter and wet early spring to final play between Joe's Capri, the home team, and the Dark Knight Lounge, the Cat's crudely assorted on-again, off-again group of Northside old-timers. They had outlasted a dozen teams, and some of their earlier opponents watched, groggy from booze and hastily made side bets that instantly turned bad. Felix and his pals struggled to show why they were the best.

I was in the Capri as a spectator, a fan of the sport that was more strategic than poker and could be more violent than bullfighting. Felix claimed I was the team's lawyer, "just in case."

The truth is, I had nothing better to do with my time. My practice kept me jumping and I had only an occasional break for entertainment. I was grateful for that. My recent office move made me concentrate on dozens of details that I had put aside for months. I was finally making real money in my chosen profession—it had taken only twenty-some years—but there I was, busy and harried, a brown, slightly worn version of a workaholic. I cared about the impression I made at bar meetings, contemplated bringing in a young attorney to help with the load, and worried about whether my socks matched my tie.

My social life suffered, a casualty of my novel professional respectability. Never the talk of the town in the first place, it had dwindled to an occasional dinner or movie with women who treated me as a brother, or an escort, certainly not a lover. An evening watching Felix's pool game sounded harmless enough.

From the beginning of the match, Felix sensed that the Dark Knight Lounge was in trouble. He had split his first two games.

Squirrel, a crazy biker who brought two guys with big biceps and filthy T-shirts for protection from the rowdies he expected in Chicano bars, was off his game. He was stoned. That normally didn't make any difference in his shooting, but his shots were just a little slow, his stick too much on the inside of the cue ball, and so he fell short, or missed by a hair. He lost two games.

Hawk-nosed Chief was clobbered in his first game by Ace García, the finest shot on the Westside. He evened up in the second round, but Chief sleep-walked through the motions. Ace had shown him how to shoot and now there was no doubt in anybody's mind who was best, but Chief had to keep playing. He drank more beer than he should, slouched in his booth, and waited in the dark for his final chance.

Fat, dependable Ray and Tony, the playboy plumber, won their games; at the end of the first two sets, the Dark Knight Lounge surprisingly had the advantage. But there was trouble in the game, there was a bad feeling in the night, and they were on the Westsiders' turf. Felix toyed with the tip of his cue and absentmindedly rubbed chalk dust in his hair when he stood to take his turn.

He turned to me and complained, "Louie, you know Westsiders. They always hassle you if you beat them. Their damn women and the punks that hang around, they're the ones. Get rid of them and we could make it out of here without a fight."

"Gato, what's worse, winning or losing?"

He shrugged. The crowd cheered only for the Capri players.

Felix misplayed his roll and had no position for the eight. His young opponent, a slick, greasy-looking guy in a shiny blue Mylar jacket with JOE'S CAPRI LOUNGE written across the back in orange script, eased the cue ball across the table, tapped the black eight ever so softly, and, as it fell, whistled just loud enough for the Cat to hear. It dropped safely in the corner pocket that had eluded Felix for most of the game. I waited for the trumpets and a hundred charging horses, but there was no cavalry to the rescue and Felix the Cat had to stretch his hand across to the winner's waiting flat palm. He passed the ten-dollar bill that had made the game ten dollars more interesting. The slick kid said, "Nice game, bro," but Felix had given it to him.

He answered, more for the crowd than the kid, "Sure, man. Hell of a shot."

Chief never got into his last game. He had four shots

and made only two balls. Felix mumbled that he hoped Chief quit the team.

But then, to prove that eight ball was made for men who believe in irony and deception, Tony played the best pool of his strung out, uptight life and wiped out 'Mando.

Felix sat with me at a shaky table where empty beer bottles rattled. In the saloon's shadows, his green eyes squinted in frustration. He had been distracted for most of the night. Something, or someone, perched on his mind like a vulture on a graveyard fence. It was a struggle, but whatever it was, he kept to himself. He talked about the players.

" 'Mando's over the hill. Too bad and real sad, because I can remember when the old goat was smooth as ice. He made five thousand in one game and then dropped it at the dog races the same night. Later, the old man told me, 'I'm just a crazy *viejo* from the Valley, and one of these days I'm going home.' The guy should have left last week."

Then Ray blew it. He scratched the eight on a simple, short, straight-in shot, the kind you hate to have to make to win, because they never drop, they won't fall, and you can say only stupid things like "too much green" or "too straight, man." Ray stared wide-eyed at the cue ball as it bounced around the table and then rolled into the side, his pudgy fingers tightening around the stick in a stranglehold. He stood up and walked out without a word, climbed in his pickup, and drove home, where he had the worst fight of his long marriage to Helen. Someone said that Ray Charles could have made that shot, but that was long after Fat Ray had trashed the kitchen and Helen had broken his pool stick by smashing it against his beer-can collection.

Ray's choke meant Squirrel had to play Ace, the man who laid it on the line in these tournaments, the man who gave no quarter to ragtag pickup players. The whole damn tournament, the months of playing every loudmouthed pool player who could afford the twenty-five bucks entry fee, the cheap beer, and the Tuesday-morning hang-overs—the whole damn mess came down to the spaced-out Hell's Angel reject who didn't know what the score was, much less that winning the trophy was dumped right on his scrawny, pink-meated, bony shoulders.

Felix ordered a shot and a beer and decided it was time for serious drinking. I had to agree. The match was over. Only the formality of losing remained.

Tony rushed up to our table from the hazy grayness of the bar.

"Squirrel's nowhere around. Where the fuck can he be?"

Felix looked at me and his eyes glinted as if he had just cashed in a winning trifecta ticket.

"Out back, toking up. Where else? You better drag him in here before we forfeit. The Capri guys are getting anxious."

He was a mouse sniffing a trap.

"Assholes."

Tony walked through the back door and into the alley.

The tension in the bar made it difficult to suck in any oxygen and I told myself I was reacting to the smoke. The Westsiders knew they had the game. It was wrapped up. They wanted it to end quickly, stop the suffering, start the party. Get it on, man! They gave Felix five minutes to have his next shooter at the table or that was it, brother—the end. Premature climax, no long, drawn-out final act. The bartender tapped another keg and dropped five dollars in the music box. Westside, forever!

Tony marched in and Squirrel followed, grinning from ear to ear. Tony whispered as he guided Squirrel to the table.

"That shitface didn't even know it was his turn. Too much! I'll kill him if he screws up."

Squirrel's abrupt appearance was an insult to the crowd. They had started the celebration, and now it had to be delayed because the missing player had decided to show up, finally, and they had to sit through one more game, one more detour on the long road to the Capri's trophy, one more of life's little hassles that made a person want to cut something up, or at least break a few chairs. The mood was nasty.

Felix made himself comfortable. He gulped beer and sipped at Jim Beam and made sure he had a cue stick near.

"Nothing left but to get drunk."

That made me worry. Felix could be a mean drunk. Alcohol stirred up drumbeats from the different jungles he had known in his forty-four years. They rumbled in his ears, blocking out sense and forbearance.

I injected a bit of strategic planning. "We better go somewhere else, then. I don't see too many faces I know, and even fewer friendly ones. Jesus, you guys are really outnumbered."

Otis and Carla, singing "Tramp," blasted from the jukebox.

I had to comment. "These Westsiders, all they know is oldies. I wonder if they ever listen to anything that was recorded after 1965?"

Felix knew. "That song came out in '67, but who's counting?"

Squirrel broke the rack and the game started.

Both players were stiff, Squirrel from the cold alley and Ace from the wait. I silently hoped that Squirrel would loosen his bones, at least give Garcia a run for his money. Slowly, the biker warmed up.

It was one of those games. Shots were made that wouldn't be duplicated again in five, ten years. The people who saw that game always talked about it later in language you knew if you grew up playing pool or hung around with guys from the streets. They talked about it in the joint, at the all-night keg parties in the projects, and in

15

the early-morning hours when young men were coming down from the night's high, the last story before home. It was the Capri game, the night Ace and Squirrel squared off, that time on the Westside.

Ace was smooth. He shot fast and hard, and he knew his groove was good. But Squirrel stuck with Ace and when he got his chance, he took it.

Squirrel made a bank shot off one of the side cushions and García clicked his teeth. Squirrel's next shot required precise placement of the cue ball for the sharp angle needed to make the ten spin and drop in the far corner. He made it.

The crowd squirmed at each of Squirrel's shots. He had been reborn. He was slapping the hands of fate and the crowd could feel the change.

Squirrel bopped around the table, singing "Otis, you a tramp," beaming like a goddamned clown, making shots as if he was in a Paul Newman movie. He hitched up his knee to the beat of the song in his head, and his spas-modic jerks around the table, Squirrel's idea of dancing, brought smirks of pity to the faces in the crowd. He scratched the back of his neck and shook his long, fusty ponytail out from under his cracked leather cap. He delib-erately, slowly chalked his stick. He licked his lips at Con-nie Muñoz, a dark-haired, chubby member of the Ace García fan club who only wanted to go down on Ace once, if she could ever get him away from Sherry Valdez.

Connie clearly considered Squirrel trash. We could hear the descriptive expressions of her opinions across the room.

"That guy makes me sick, baby. Can't you do anything about him? Look, he keeps eyeing me, giving me that *baboso* smile. Yech, what a creep. I wish you would do something."

Her date was part-time thief, full-time cocaine freak Chopper García, no relation to Ace, and he had enough beer, schnapps, and assorted pharmaceuticals in him to believe Connie, something he had previously avoided.

Squirrel lined up for the shot that could win the game. He bent down to the edge of the green and peered across the table at the easy lie of the cue ball and the eight. He knew he was going to make it. He could see the ball score after he gave it his slow, smooth stroke.

We watched with uneasy fascination. Squirrel could make the shot, but we weren't sure he should.

Connie whined to her date that the *gabacho* was a perverted pest.

"God! He's trying to make a pass at me right in the middle of the game with Ace."

I saw it happen and I swear to this day that there was nothing I could do about it. I was paralyzed in my chair, a witness to a scene that only Rod Serling might have enjoyed, but it froze me for an instant and that's all it took.

Chopper staggered to his feet and reached for Squirrel's stick. It was his obligation, his Westside duty. He had to tell the honky hippie that no one could beat Ace on his own table. No Westsider would allow it. And he had to tell the guy to leave Connie alone. I could read drunken Chopper's thoughts, etched in the sweat of his olive forehead— You can't act that way around our women.

And just when Chopper was about to make the grandest gesture of his meager existence, he tripped over Connie's foot and fell into Squirrel's arm. Squirrel lurched forward. His cue, a five-foot extension of his body, noisily sliced the table and left a gash a yard long.

Squirrel's arm jerked to the right. After ruining the table, his stick slammed the cue ball and sent it flying across the ravaged felt and onto the floor. Squirrel angrily pushed away the interloper. The realization of what had happened set in, and he wasn't sure what he should do. Then he casually stomped on Chopper's fingers. Chopper squealed like a cat caught in a screen door.

17

Connie screamed, jumped to her feet, and knocked her long-neck beer bottle to the floor. Beer and glass erupted in a small explosion. The crowd recognized the pop of another one wasted. Connie grabbed a ball from the table and threw it at Squirrel with a vicious toss from only six feet away.

Squirrel's head bounced with the force of the impact, his eyes rolling back in his head. He slowly pivoted toward the woman, whipped his stick at her face, and cracked it across her forehead.

All hell broke loose then.

3

Cora Lee Hawkins and her husband, Jessee, tried not to stare at the bruise puffing up my right eye, but it was no use. The blue-black glob strained for attention, and my client and her soon-to-be ex-husband obliged. They had experience in these matters and graciously offered advice to reduce the swelling, everything from ice packs and raw steak to mud from Sloan Lake. I didn't resist the information. I could tell they knew what they were talking about. Cora Lee's black eye was almost gone and Jessee's had lapsed into that yellow-gray stage that, as Cora Lee explained, "looks obnoxious but don't hardly hurt no more."

Black eyes seemed to be the order of the day. I was in Courtroom 18 with Ms. Hawkins to finalize her divorce from Jessee. The urgency of the dissolution had been punctuated by the latest exchange of blows between the couple, and I guess it was only right that the lawyer should wear a shiner in solidarity with his client. So there we stood before Judge Clark, three bruised and battered human beings going through the litany of permanent orders, my head bursting at the seams, Cora Lee too choked up to do much except whimper, and Jessee sullen and quiet, not quite sure what else the judge would do to him in addition to yanking away his wife.

While waiting for our turn with the judge, my client had asked about my injury, and I had hemmed and hawed about a garage door. The truth was that I had been smacked in the head with a beer bottle during the blowout at the Capri, but I figured Cora Lee was strung out enough without hearing about the trouble her lawyer managed to find the week of her court appearance.

I was thankful that there weren't a lot of people in the courtroom, just about a dozen of my colleagues who found it very interesting that I had once again appeared in court in a manner a notch or two below dignified.

"Nice eye, Montez."

"Trouble collecting your fee, Louie?"

Or just a shake of the head and a glassy stare.

Melissa Ralston sat in front of the judge's bench, diligently recording the proceedings for posterity. She usually performed her role in the state's judicial system with a somber and brusque attitude, although beneath her tiny table and frenetic stenographic machine she managed to wear skirts short enough to distract the Charlie Manson jury. For the Hawkins divorce, she exhibited the biggest grin I had seen since the latest rerun of "Mister Ed." When at last the hearing was over and Cora Lee was emancipated, Melissa couldn't contain herself any longer. She rushed from the courtroom into the clerk's office. Laughter from behind the clerk's door followed me as I guided Cora Lee out of the courtroom.

Jessee stopped us at the elevator.

"Say, Cora Lee, can I, uh, can I talk to you for a minute? I mean, it's okay, ain't it, Montez?"

Two mother-of-pearl snaps lay unbuttoned at the top of his black-and-red western shirt, revealing a patch of light brown hair that matched the locks draping his shoulders underneath his droopy Stetson. He looked about nineteen. His *pro se* paperwork listed his age as twenty-nine.

Cora questioned me with an ache in her eyes that wanted me to say it was all right for her to talk with the man she had lived and fought with for the past five years. I shouted in my throbbing head for her to run, to jump into the elevator and catch a cab to the airport and dump this worthless bird forever before he got his hooks into her again, before he tricked her with his bright blue eyes and lazy twang, before he convinced her to have a beer, before they ended up thrashing with each other through another night of blood-boiling sex, before he lost it and slapped her around, before she came back to me, wondering what it would take to free herself.

"I don't think it's a good idea. You should just go your separate ways. If Ms. Hawkins wants to talk with you, that's up to her. But if she says for you to leave her alone, you better do it or I'll have the sheriff pick you up again, and this time you won't get out after only one night in jail. You understand?"

He wanted to squeeze my balls and make me squirm in the courthouse hallway. The blue eyes turned gray and his already-pale skin faded even more. Whiteness crept from his neck to his earlobes, and I could smell the anger he needed to unleash on me in the same way he had done to Cora Lee for years. But he only smiled, fingertipped the brim of his hat, and turned to walk away.

Cora Lee rigidly stared at me but didn't say a word. I half-pushed, half-pulled her into the elevator.

She was quiet until we were in the street.

"Well, thanks again, Mr. Montez. I couldn't have done this without you. You do something about that eye, you hear?"

She leaned over and kissed me on the cheek, then she was gone. Her perfume stayed with me as I watched and silently wished her good luck. She crossed the street and, at the corner, took a second to decide which way to go. When at last she continued, I hoped she wasn't walking in the direction of Jessee's pickup.

I yanked the ticket off my windshield and threw it on the pile of similar legal notices I filed away on the backseat. Another week and I would have to talk to the traffic-court referee and convince her that my heavy courtroom load sometimes required me to stay beyond my allotted time according to the meters. She then would knock out a few, reduce the rest, and I would give her the necessary cash just in time to avoid the notorious Denver boot.

I pulled into downtown traffic on my way to my new office near my house in northwest Denver.

The sleek, low-slung foreign job that I thought was a necessity to go along with my change of address had strained a gasket somewhere deep inside its complex and confounding high-temperature engine. It had rested in Willy Guzmán's shop for more than a week while Willy waited for parts and, I imagined, read up on how to take apart the computerlike workings of my latest status symbol. I was forced to drive my 1975 Bonneville Brougham, a car I had kept around more for sentimental reasons than anything else. The gray tank was out of style, banged up on the passenger side, ate too much gas, and leaked oil all over the environment, but at least it started up in the morning and chugged into my garage at night.

A taxi raced through the intersection at Fifteenth, trying to beat the yellow light. I silently cussed at the cabbie's idiocy. The squeal of brakes was followed by papers flying through the air, spilled from an open cab door. A black child bounced from the cab, skidded on the street, and lay, dazed, on the asphalt. The light changed and I slowly maneuvered around the boy. An older boy darted from the cab and bunched the papers in his arms. He grabbed the first kid by his elbow and dragged and carried him. He slammed the door shut and the cab spurted forward.

22

That's the way it was in the city that year—odd, out-of-kilter things that added up to a season of insanity.

Ten minutes later, I locked the car and started across the street to the office. A young man with bushy hair, an old overcoat, and army boots walked down the middle of the street, pushing a grocery cart loaded with cans, bags, bottles, and other assorted junk. He counted his steps out loud, apparently measuring the street for future reference. He made me nervous and I played with my keys in my hands. I stared, not thinking that I might attract his attention.

Without warning, the guy turned and said sweetly, "Hey, El Spicko, how you doin'?"

The kid showed his teeth in what was meant to be a smile but that came out instead as a grotesque leer because of holes in his mouth from missing canines.

The keys fell from my fingers and clanked on the asphalt. I thought I should grab him and push him around, maybe make him apologize. But all I did was flip him off. The guy pushed his cart away and I traveled back at least thirty years:

The skinny white-haired bohunk kid shouted out the words. "Son of a bitch!" He stood with hands on his hips, lips curled into a mean snarl. Louie stared away, looked into the dirt before he answered. "Shut up." The kid laughed and walked away. Then he turned and shouted, "Mexican son of a bitch!" Louie didn't know what to do. Was he expected to fight the kid for saying such a dumb thing, or what? He looked toward his house. She stood on the porch. She said, "He's talking about me, your mother. How come you don't do anything?" The kid was gone.

The junk collector's voice brought me back. "Hey, man. I didn't know. You know, I saw the tie and suit, and I just

23

thought, well, you know. So, okay, screw it. Here, man, here, I'm sorry."

He raised his ass and wiggled in a way so vulgar that my stomach tightened. He ran to the end of the block.

He shouted, "I'm sorry, already. I'm stupid. What can I say? How am I supposed to know?"

The guy ran, pushing his cart, weaving through the downtown traffic. I stared helplessly from the curb at his back, my finger pointed to the sky, outstretched in the clear morning air, an insignificant response to the insult hurled from nowhere, out of ignorance.

I dropped my hand and tried to shake out the uneasiness. I told myself he was just a freak, a loser at the bad beginning of a bad day and I shouldn't let him get to me. Look at all the good I had going for me.

Gloria hadn't demanded an increase in child support for months, and that in and of itself was a welcome relief. But what was crucial was that she hadn't called to complain about the boys' school or the cheat who worked on her plumbing or the latest catastrophe in her immediate family of nine aunts, four uncles, thirty-five cousins, two sets of grandparents, and a mother who squandered all her Social Security on items Gloria considered meaningless—hats, magazines, beer.

I had more divorce work than I really cared for, and I had managed to find a couple of slip-and-falls that looked as if they might actually pay. And my juices were steaming because of the Jenny Rodríguez lawsuit.

I had filed a complaint against Denver's finest for the beating Jenny had suffered at the hands of zealous cops who got sidetracked on a routine drug bust. They'd unleashed their clubs and sent her to the hospital. There was no doubt in my mind that Jenny would be paid by the city; it was only a question of how much. I was the guy who would resolve that little matter, for about a quarter of the take, and that knowledge made me enjoy my work again.

Evangelina gave me a perfunctory "Good morning, boss," then handed me three message slips. She stared at my eye and started to say something, then simply shook her head.

"Evie, how long you been my secretary?"

"Too long, Louie."

"That's exactly what I was thinking."

Before she gave me a smart response, I turned to the messages.

Gary Yarbrough from the City Attorney's Office called about scheduling Jenny's deposition. I smiled. Jenny would make a good strong witness. If the city attorney needed an excuse to make an offer, he would find it in the solid, unimpeachable testimony of my client.

My father had made the second call. I spoke to Evangelina without looking up.

"Evie, remind me to call Jesús."

She scribbled a note on the large desk calendar she kept to help me organize my business life.

The final piece of paper contained a message from Felix. I left Evangelina in the waiting room and tried to get comfortable in my freshly painted office. I discarded my suit coat and dug out the Hawkins file from my briefcase. As I made notes in the file about the hearing and what Jessee had said after court, I tried to guess what Felix might want. I hadn't heard from the guy twice in one week since we were young goofballs on the prowl for good times. When I finished tying up the strings of Cora Lee's divorce, I called him at his store.

He answered his phone with a lethargic "¿Qué dices, narices?"—which meant that I had to respond with a lukewarm "Nada, cagada." He acted as though he didn't recognize me, making me go through the routine of announcing my identity. After a minute or so of mumbles and silence, I reminded him that he had called me and I was merely returning his message.

My renewed energy for the practice of law meant less time for old friends. I didn't have the requisite ambition to drink and carouse, as any relationship with the guys would have required. My interlude at the Capri had shown me the validity of my theory that playing with Felix could be harmful to my business and my health. So I was only slightly interested when he asked if I wanted to have a few beers. For Felix, "a few beers" was anything less than one wall of his liquor store. My hesitation meant more than that I was thinking about it, and Felix knew me well enough to figure out that my heart wasn't into another all-nighter.

His deep voice asked me to reconsider.

"I don't mean that we have to tear it up, Louie. It's been a tough week, a real tough day. I could use a little time to stretch out, maybe talk."

I doubted that we would do much talking.

"Just a beer or two, man. I have to have a clear head tomorrow. You know how it is."

"Sure, whatever. The Denver around eight?"

"Just a few beers, Felix."

I returned to business. Clients and opposing counsel called on a half dozen cases, but nothing surprising. The best call of the day came from Larry Olguín, barrio artist, guitarist, and lead singer for the local band Cariño Nuevo. He wanted to let me know about his latest cultural endeavors. I had become something of a groupie for the band. They were a tight outfit, making a name in the weekly neighborhood paper as a good, entertaining Chicano band, and it was only a matter of time before they released a cassette for their fans.

"*Oye*, Louie. The band will be at the J. P. Martínez Legion Hall on Sunday afternoon—a fund-raiser for their scholarship fund. Five bucks to get in, then you buy beer, burritos, so on and so forth. You know the routine. Why not, hey? Good cause and all that, and we get to kick around a few jams."

"Still playing oldies, Larry?"

"What else is there? Rock and roll, slow dances, and, of course, classic *corridos* and *rancheras*. But we're throwing in a few of our own songs. Bobby Modesto, the keyboard player, has written two numbers that get a good response. Check us out. The crowd at these things has a nice mix. *Pura gente, tu sabes. Ancianos,* younger couples, even a few women looking for a man who knows how to dance. Maybe you'll get lucky. Try to drop by."

"Thanks. I'll see what I can do. When's your next gallery show?"

Larry had painted for years. One of his murals had graced a recreation center wall before graffiti, a new mayor, and time had reduced it to a jumbled, faded blankness. I tried to make it to Larry's shows whenever he managed to get some space to hang his work. Larry had introduced me to his group of artist friends, who somehow created art in the middle of a city that either ignored or humored them.

"Ain't got nothing going. Hate to admit it, but the band has kept me away from the easel. Not sure I got it anymore. Hey, but María Aguirre hung some of her stuff at the Guadalupe *tiendita,* off of Larimer and Twenty-first. She's dynamite, man. Beautiful arrangements. Incorporates Chicano myths with images of urban decay—*la llorona* hanging out on the corner with miniskirted *chamacas, el coco* low-riding. That kind of feel. Give it a look."

"Later. Thanks."

A few hours passed while I read through files, dictated letters and memos, and asked Evie to schedule or reschedule meetings or appointments. I was a well-oiled litigating machine, deep into research and trial strategy, when I heard the rustle of a dress and a faked cough.

Evangelina stared at me from my desk lamp, worried

27

and troubled. I rocked on the back legs of my chair and waited for her to say something. I hadn't seen her look so unsure of herself since the day she'd interviewed for the job. The gamble I had taken on her had paid off in spades.

"Louie, Jenny just called. There's something she needs to talk to you about, but she's not ready yet. She's not, uh, sure she wants to go through with it . . . with the case, now."

I almost fell out of my seat as I slammed the chair to the floor.

"What? What's wrong? We've just started. The city is going to make an offer. She's got to be patient. What happened?"

Evie's hands twisted around a piece of tissue and she had a hard time looking at me. She had warned me about getting involved with her family. In fact, she had talked to me before I agreed to represent Jenny and wanted it clearly understood that she was not pressuring me to take the case. It should make no difference, she'd said, that Jenny was her stepsister.

"Louie, I tried to tell you. Jenny and her brothers and sisters have been around; they know the score. They leave me pretty much alone, but they took care of me when I needed help. And they're my father's kids, too."

She was having an uncharacteristically difficult time getting to the point.

"Some of them are pretty wild. You know Jenny; you've talked to her. She's done about everything. I've seen her beat up guys twice her size who tried to hurt her or someone she cares about."

I believed it. It had taken four policemen to subdue Jenny the night of what I had been calling "the incident."

"Anyway, she's worried that her case is going to make it tough on the people she knows, especially Victor. She would do anything for her boy—my nephew—but he's a punk as far as I'm concerned. To Jenny, he's God's little angel. She wants out because of him."

"I don't get it, Evie. What does her son have to do with her case against the city? The cops and their clubs, gas, and dogs really jacked up some people. They should pay for what they did. What gives?"

My investigation had turned up the unsurprising fact that the bust of the Intangible Club had come down because an informant had provided trustworthy information on the dealing that was going on in the after-hours joint—trustworthy enough for a warrant. And everybody knew about the underage drinking.

Jenny had been in the club, but she had every right. They didn't find anything on her and when she fought back against their so-called searches, they beat her. It turned into a police riot. The crowd squared off against the police in the club's parking lot and the adjoining park. Tear gas poisoned the downtown air. The dogs chased terrified people down alleys and across streets. Jenny's case was one of a dozen filed against the city.

"That's all Jenny told me. For you to drop the case, and when I pushed her for a reason, she said only that Victor was in enough trouble. She's stubborn, Louie. She wouldn't tell me anything else. I'm sorry."

She stared at my Aztec wall calendar.

It took me a minute or so to come up with something to say. I wanted to jump up and vent my frustration at Evie, but not only did that not make any sense; it would have cost me a damn good secretary. Evie and Jenny were like *menudo* and *posole;* the similarities were obvious enough but the subtle differences were critical. Evie was as solid as Mother Earth; Jenny an unknown moon rock.

"I'll have to talk with Ms. Rodríguez. It's not as easy as she thinks to just walk away from a lawsuit against the city and county of Denver. We filed the complaint, argued against the city's motion to dismiss, and convinced the

29

judge to put the case on his accelerated docket. There's a pretrial in a few weeks, and the city attorney handling the case called this morning. He probably wants to schedule a depo. It's not over, not yet."

Evie shrugged and threw her tissue in my wastebasket. On her way out, she said, "Be careful, Louie."

Right. Now I had to deal with the Chicana Wonder Woman, and, if my hunch was correct, I would end up trying to find my way out of all the twisted and gnarled roots and branches of the Rodríguez family tree. *¡Ay, raza!* Just when I thought life had taken a turn down El Camino Real. Suddenly, the golden highway was as dark and cluttered as a potholed Northside alley.

4

I-70 cut through the foothills west of town and up into the front range. My beleaguered Bonneville, a few years beyond its prime, gasped as I tried to keep it going past Dead Man's Curve and into the historic mining-town counties. I'm a jaded city boy, and in Colorado, postcard vistas are almost too common, but driving from Denver into the Rocky Mountains is one of the best for me. As the billboards used to say, " 'Tis a privilege to live in Colorado." Colorado is one of the states in Aztlán, by the way. When we demanded the return of the Chicano homeland, we weren't talking only about the deserts of Arizona, New Mexico, or Texas. *¡Orale, ése!*

And if lush rivers, verdant meadows, and snow-capped, cloud-crowned peaks don't quite cut it, welcome to the high country gaming rooms. The mellow, usually reserved state of Colorado had suffered an attack of gambling fever not matched since the Fifty-niners bet their lives on striking it rich in the mountain streams. Blackjack, poker, and slot machines were legalized in selected mountain towns, with the hope that they would revive the tepid tourist trade. What could be the harm in a few slots and a poker table or two inside the curio shops? Well, the shops were gone, but in their place were casinos packed with high rollers, medium rollers, and plenty of low rollers bent on taking as much gold out of the towns as any prospector ever did. Laid-back gift boutiques that previously had offered pyrite nuggets, jackalope wood carvings and a half hour of gold panning turned into glitzy gambling emporiums and five-dollar-an-hour parking lots.

Central City, Cripple Creek, Black Hawk—almost gone but not forgotten.

Sure, I can get into odds, bets, and good-luck charms as much as the next guy, especially for limited-stakes gambling. But I don't have a jones about it, and I had my doubts about what really had been accomplished. I might have regretted the loss of the quaint tourist traps, except that—surprise, surprise—legalized gambling meant more business for lawyers. And I was small *papas* in this league. I could only guess at the take in the massive downtown firms. One thing about my profession—a business person doesn't necessarily need *money* to make money, but lawyers are an absolute must.

So I hadn't been totally taken aback when Douglas Brindle, a Seventeenth Street lawyer, talked to me about helping him close a real estate opportunity in Central City. He needed a negotiator, someone to do the running around for one of his clients who wanted to pick up a hunk of the still-available land in Central City. Brindle expected to finish the transaction and set up the casino when the land was safely in his client's pocket and he had figured out a way to get around the recent moratorium on new casinos. Because Brindle and I had worked together on small business ventures and he trusted my instincts about deals, he had offered me the chance to do the initial dirty work. He wanted to keep his firm out of the up-front talks, just in case.

Brindle had explained my role one day over afternoon

cappuccino at a downtown coffee shop recently imported from Seattle. The guy knew how to dress, and I envied that. His tie was brighter than the courthouse Christmas lights, and just as inspirational. The color scheme matched the pattern in his suit, and over it all lay the thin, pleasing aroma of a real man's aftershave. If I didn't know myself better, I could have been a law student infatuated with the partner who offered a summer internship. I made a mental note to buy some new ties.

"Talk with the seller. See where he's coming from. He wants more than a million for a couple of lots bordering Central City and Black Hawk—and they may be worth it. But Nulan, my client, has to get permission from the commissioners to build the damn casino. There's so much red tape that it could cost another hundred grand easy just to set it up. It's a long shot—all the media backlash about unfulfilled promises and the quality of life and the usual kind of small-mind bickering by those who aren't lucky enough to be in on the action. We could end up with land that can't be used for anything except a parking lot. And you know that's not where the real money is."

"Sure, Doug, whatever you say. You want me to talk to this guy Edwin Talmage for your client, soften him up while you check out the licenses, permits, et cetera, et cetera. He knows I'm involved?"

"He will. I'll call him. Officially, you're looking into the offer just like any other potential buyer or buyer's representative. But you can't close anything out for Nulan, you understand that?"

"I'm working for you, Doug. You're paying me by the hour to talk to the seller and tell you what I learn. If he asks, I'll tell him that. Okay?"

Doug reached across the table and shook my hand.

I made one more point. "This casino business isn't exactly what people expected, Doug. Only a few are making real money. Why the sudden interest?"

"There's always a buck to be made, Louie. Nulan wants to take a chance and he's got the dough. He'll make money. Those kind of guys always do."

I had to agree with that. The gift-shop and grocery-store owners who thought gambling might mean a secure retirement probably would end up gasping for financial air in the rarified atmosphere of Colorado's big risk. The men with money in the first place would simply make more money and then move on to other projects. Brindle finished his instructions.

"Talmage is tough, Louie. Tough and incredibly rich. Made his money in construction, real estate, computers. He was in at the beginning of almost every kind of enterprise in the past thirty years that really paid off. A money-making genius, in the right spot at the right time. And here he is again, holding a piece of land that five years ago he picked up for next to nothing, that he couldn't give away, and now we're talking to him about that same bit of dirt, seriously thinking about a million bucks. I doubt he'll budge on his price, but there's no harm in asking. He lives up there in a house specially built for him, all kinds of fancy gadgets to make it easier on him. He's in a wheelchair, you know? Ever since his stroke a few years back."

I nodded. I knew more about Mr. Talmage than Doug guessed. My good friend Felix the Cat had once been married to Mr. Talmage's only daughter, Martha. I hoped that piece of information could be used at the right time, as long as I could recognize that time when it popped up.

Now, several weeks later, Evangelina had passed through Brindle's call, a few minutes after I had finished grumbling about Jenny's unfortunate decision. Talmage expected me that afternoon, at his place.

"Be prompt, Louie. Talmage won't put up with tardiness."

"No problem. I'll leave now so I can be up there in plenty

of time. How about black eyes? You think Talmage will mind if I bring one along?"

"What are you jabbering about?"

"Never mind. Fax me the papers I need. Then I'll take off."

"They're on their way. Good luck, Louie."

I had reviewed the paperwork, rescheduled a few appointments, and then took off for the mountains. There hadn't been time to call Felix and get the lowdown on his former father-in-law, so I'd decided to play it by ear. I could always talk to Felix later and learn what I needed to know, if there were to be any future meetings with Talmage.

I exited the highway, got on the main road into Central City, and from there to another, tougher path that in the winter had to require four-wheel drive. My tank shook and groaned as dust billowed behind me, the wake of the out-of-place Pontiac. Talmage's house sat back from the road, and I didn't see any driveway. I parked my car with the hope that no one took the curve too quickly. Anyone doing more than ten miles an hour didn't have a prayer of avoiding the fenders and bumper of what once had been a stylish mode of travel.

A sidewalk from the road changed into a ramp that led up to the door; no steps. A weather-beaten sign hung near the door: TRI-AGE MANAGEMENT. I reached down to a doorbell set at about knee level and was answered by the barking of at least three different dogs. A tall man in a flannel shirt, faded denim pants, and scruffy boots opened the door. He smiled at my black eye. I gave him my card and waited. A pair of slobbering Dobermans sniffed my tightly clenched hands.

By the time Cheap Jeans returned, the dogs had taken to licking my shoes.

"Come in. Mr. Talmage waits in the library."

I followed him through a house that could have been a set for a fantastic movie about little people with wheels for

35

feet. Talmage had used some of his money to provide the easiest access for his chair. The rest of us had to manage in whatever way we could—a sentiment I'm sure he'd experienced firsthand.

Extrawide doorways opened into rooms with what at first appeared to be miniature tables, chairs, windows, and shelves. Eventually, I realized that the furniture was regular size, but it all sat close to the floor, within reach of a man condemned to a rolling prison only inches above the ground. There were no stairs in the house.

The "library" was nothing more than a busy, obviously well-used office. I didn't see a single book. My host sat in the middle of the room, surrounded by a desk covered with files, architects' plans, letters, contracts, and other such debris that millionaires must accumulate while they think up schemes for more money. There was one soft spot—a framed studio portrait of a pretty, smiling blond woman sitting next to a dark-haired, equally smiling young girl.

My card, conveniently handy in case he forgot my name, protruded from a groove in one of the arms on his chair.

He wore a green-and-white exercise outfit, athletic shoes, and a Colorado Rockies baseball cap perched on his bald head. His left hand twisted around a silver control knob on the chair, while his right hung useless at his side. His scrawny neck rigidly stayed at one angle, but his eyes moved incessantly, from me to his papers, to his assistant, back to me. He looked anything but disabled.

The man got right to the point. Apparently, I didn't need to explain that I didn't actually represent anybody.

"I want a million and a quarter for the parcels. I told Brindle that months ago. If he waits much longer, the price will go up. Nulan and I have done business before. I don't know why he thinks he needs to drag in all these, these, uh, lawyers."

He grimaced at me as if I had one eye hanging loose.

"Mr. Talmage, I'm here only to collect information. There must be a way to do business that will benefit all concerned. It's just that, with the moratorium, the commissioners backing off from more development, and the end of the gambling honeymoon, there may be room to work something out on the terms, the price, the . . ."

He rolled toward me, and I wasn't sure he intended to stop before he crunched my toes with his wheels. He glanced at my card.

"Montez. Don't waste my time. I know what Nulan has to do to build his casino. So does he. He should have jumped on my offer when I first made it. His stalling only hurt him. I hope he didn't wait because of advice from his lawyers. But my price is firm. You, or Brindle at least, should have all the documents. The details are spelled out there. Get Nulan to sign, send me a check on the first installment, and he can start greasing whomever he has to. That's not my concern. I'm in real estate. I buy and sell land. Anything else?"

He picked up a stack of papers from his desk and scanned them with the clear message that he had finished with me. Whatever it was about the deal, or Nulan, or Brindle, or, most likely, me, I had not scored any points. I tried to make a graceful exit.

"Well, I'm sorry we couldn't talk more. Maybe some other time, all of us together, dinner, whatever."

He almost smiled at my ludicrous proposition, then turned back to his papers.

I guess he had rattled me. I was on my way out, and I could have retreated with some dignity, some semblance of business as usual, even if it was a little rough. But I had to take one more shot, leave him with something personal to think about so that maybe next time he would loosen his sphincter and act a bit more human. That's when I violated one of Professor Younger's Ten Commandments of Cross-Examination—I asked a question I didn't know the answer to, that one question too many:

"Say, you seen Felix Guerrero lately?"

He didn't turn red, roll his eyes, or thrash about in his wheelchair. In fact, physically, all he did was mutter a curse, "Son of a bitch," followed by an order to his aide, "Johnny, show him the door!" But there was a feeling in that room that spooked the attempt to be personal right out of me. The mention of Felix's name created some kind of chemical reaction. I smelled sulfur and tasted bile, and twangs of something not quite fear but on the other side of paranoia traveled up my spine. I had felt that before, years ago in college, during an all-night mescaline binge with a few friends and a mob of strangers. An eccentric, spaced-out free-love apostle had inspired such nerve-racking suspicion in me that I'd left in a panic. He turned out to be wanted for particularly brutal rapes and assaults.

On Talmage's porch, as Johnny shut the door behind me, I forced thin mountain air into my lungs and decided I needed a drink, at least.

The drive into Central City took only a few minutes. Finding a parking spot in a lot on a hill far from the action, riding a bus into the heart of the town, and finally propping myself on a bar stool at the Ton O' Gold Saloon and Casino took considerably longer.

The late-afternoon slot customers reminded me of any Las Vegas crowd—solemn and methodical. Where was the fun? The repetitive play hypnotized me as I watched thousands of dollars disappear into the blinking, noisy machines in a matter of minutes. I wandered around the bar, still uneasy from my encounter with Talmage. I strolled through three floors of slots, blackjack and poker tables, and an empty restaurant.

I exchanged a few bills for rolls of quarters from a change girl and tried to be scientific about picking a machine. There must be signs that a payoff is due on the very next quarter. Nothing clear came to mind, so I sat down at a machine that pictured a bikini-clad cowgirl riding the backseat of a red convertible. Red could have been my lucky color. The spin paid nothing, so I did it again. A few quarters plunked into the tray, so I did it again. That was about the time I noticed the man standing behind me.

Is it just me, or what? There is an ugly mood out there, let me tell you, and that year crazy things just happened. What could I do when the evil-looking skinhead—leathers, weird hair, weirder eyes—tapped me on the shoulder while I tried to make three sevens in a row—PAYOFF = 1,250 COINS—and said, "Are you a Jew?"

His eyes were glazed over, red and tiny, and he scratched an iron cross tattooed across his wrist. He looked as if he'd crawled out from under the nearest toilet seat.

Like an idiot, I tried to answer him. I actually tried to explain to him that no, I wasn't Jewish, but what exactly was he?

Of course, he said, "I'm an American."

He growled. A wimpy smile escaped his thin lips, as if he had issued some kind of challenge, as if I was supposed to say, Well, excuse my ass, I didn't know I was in freaking America. I'm from Iraq myself, so why don't you get your pals and torture me, jerk?

I didn't say that, naturally. My answer was cool.

"I'm an American, too."

God, he looked as though he'd crapped his dirty jeans right there and could feel it oozing down his legs and into his boots. He found his voice and gave me a classic line he must have memorized for the occasion.

"Fuck you, you mongrel motherfucker!"

I grabbed him, pushed him around, shook him a little. He grabbed me back, started shaking me, and in a couple of quick eye blinks we were both waltzing around like two kids at the prom. People were shouting, the lights reeled above us, and we were having a great time. It was almost enough to get Talmage out of my system.

One of the security guys ran toward us. I saw him huffing and puffing, his wide washboard forehead turning red and his cheeks billowing, while I gave my buddy a hard, vicious shove into the next row of slots. He hit them like a bull. That started something I still don't understand. The slots began to ring and whistle, making all kind of noise, and the guard got this real worried look on his face.

The guard tried to turn off a machine that was going ape-shit. It kept turning, blinking, and whirring. It sounded as if it was going to explode, so he lost interest in us temporarily. The creep made it back to his feet. He rubbed his head and groaned. The Central City Welcome Wagon reached into his back pocket and whipped out a knife, and I knew I had dropped into something that was bigger than both of us.

Maybe the Ton O' Gold spent some real money on security. Maybe there had been so much negative publicity about gambling that the casino owners had instructed their people to take affirmative steps to keep things at a sociable level. Maybe the guard liked his work. Whatever it was, he surprised me. He tore into Colonel Klink before I had any clue as to what I was going to do. The guard let him have it with a fist wrapped around a roll of quarters, and that was it. The skinhead dropped to his knees, his eyes did the bugaloo inside his head for a second, then he fell forward onto the nice carpet those places have—and good night, sweetheart.

And me, I jumped, too—right into the pile of quarters that streamed out of the machine the security guard had tried to keep quiet. But I wasn't the only one. You'd think that in Central City, where after about thirty minutes money loses all meaning and the reason everybody acts like maniacs is because they want to win—it doesn't matter how much, just win, man—you'd think people could accept thousands of quarters pouring out of a machine gone crazy. The besieged security guard tried to protect his boss's money, but there was too much silver, too much, and we all wanted our own pocketful of the stuff.

That's when I got hurt. There was this woman, nice-looking, too, just a little old for me, wearing a spangly dress and smelling good and obviously one over her limit of vodka tonics, and she kicked me right in the kidneys with her high heels, hard. I rubbed my back all the way home.

5

Gato and I had grown up together in the parks, basketball courts, and rec halls of the Northside. Cruising downtown, we made the scene on Sixteenth Street, where every Denver kid with any kind of wheels managed to end up on Friday night. Nothing too intense, just a little imaginary head-butting like bantam roosters in the backyard of my grandmother's house. Eventually, we returned to our part of town, up and down Federal, through the Scotchman, more posturing and tire squeals. We dragged Thirty-eighth Avenue in our fathers' cars until we gave in to the cops stopping us every night and found new neighborhoods, new girls to chase, new rivals to stare down or outdance at all-night house parties.

Occasionally, we prowled a park with the trite name of Inspiration Point, where we could interrupt lovers, drink beer, and mumble about our futures while we looked over Lakeside Amusement Park and the mountains. We chilled out at the Point because we believed we were safe there—a peaceful hill windswept and quiet except for grunts and groans from city traffic below. The contours of the urban sprawl were outlined by moving ribbons of light from the interstate. And it was always Felix and I celebrating—talking drivel, taking a breather from the grind of Denver's Northside while we mapped out a plan for progress that was measured in good times, pretty girls, and chances to grow up quicker than we needed.

We jammed through four quick years at North High. I went off to college and the Chicano Revolution. Felix took a more popular route, at least for most of the guys I knew, and ended up doing time in a place known as the Nam. A dozen years added up before I saw him again.

Our lives had continued, through birth, death, divorce, and taxes, but we finished the circle. We somehow ended up where we'd started when we'd hugged good-bye on the high school steps the first day of our respective long, strange trips.

Drinking and partying with Felix every two or three weeks could not be a regular part of my routine for a couple of years, because I had decided I had to grow up. That meant working hard at my career and playing less with the guys. But when we needed time away from everything else, we still found each other. We could talk about the old days, scheme and dream about the future, laugh at politicians, and grumble about the crap we seemed to step in every day. We were buds, partners, homeboys, and we hung on to that.

The Denver Bar and Grill had been our place before it was legal for us to drink. I didn't know a time when it wasn't an essential part of our neighborhood. Ducktailed, loud-talking, finger-popping boys looking for big-haired, loud-talking, finger-popping girls learned how to drink in the Denver. We kept it for ourselves long after we'd passed the finger-popping stage.

Geno Lazzeri had a fetish for honky-tonk tunes that tugged at redneck heartstrings and, since he was the sole owner now that Geno Senior had made his way to the big saloon in the sky, he exercised his right to set the ambience in any fashion he wanted. A song about a Houston heartbreaker or the last time some down-and-out cowboy had a good drink, good job, and good woman floated in the background, or else it wasn't the Denver. I tried to keep it in perspective. Mexican music was just as hokey and it often had the same beat. The best local bands, including Cariño Nuevo, sprinkled in George Strait and Patsy Cline with the standard oldies and *rancheras*. The older I get, the more I recognize that there are fewer and fewer constants. One essential I can count on is that the band at any Chicano wedding dance will play "Kansas City" and "Honky-Tonk" before the lights are turned on and the gifts carried to the cars of members of the wedding party for safekeeping until the gift-opening party the next day.

Felix took his time showing up at the Denver. In his absence, I had been forced to carry on a conversation with Carla, Geno's oldest daughter. The plump, eternal teenager pumped out beer, pretzels, and giggles for her father's customers in front of an ancient smeared and cracked mirror. Naugahyde diamond stitch covered the ceiling and bar, held in place with brass buttons as big around as half-dollars. Small round tables with vinyl black-and-white checkerboard tablecloths sat empty, occupied only during the occasional lunch rush.

I had finished my first beer, gotten halfway through my second, and listened to Carla's fourth lawyer joke by the time Felix showed up.

His thick, wavy hair, as black as the day he was born, sloped backward in the same pachuco, carnival-barker style he'd picked up when he was thirteen and loose as a goose. Always bigger than I, he had about three inches and forty pounds of an advantage, the weight packed tightly around big bones. He didn't have a Chicano build, a Chicano look, or even a Chicano face, whatever those are, but there was no mistaking his heritage. A gray-blue cross tattoo twitched to the beat of his pulse on the web of his

44

left hand, rubbed down and faded after thirty years. The way his eyes lidded over when he talked assured the clique who'd grown up with him that he was stone *raza*, and I had seen him outflank adversaries with enough smarts never to doubt that he would be solid in any tough situation.

But that night, he looked bad—and not just from an unfulfilled need to recuperate from the Capri fight. Thick lines around his eyes bunched up his skin into a permanent squint. He seemed paler than I remembered, and heavier, slower. And the sadness in the famous green eyes could mean only one thing—a woman had crept into his heart and eaten a good portion of what was left of the romantic soul of my Chicano brother.

"Drink up, man. Let's go look at naked women."

I groaned. That was his cue for the Honeypot, the strip joint on the outer limits of the city, just inside Adams County, that we had patronized over the years out of habit more than anything else.

I tried to beg off.

"I'm not in the mood, Felix. I have plenty of work tomorrow, and there's nothing new out there. We always end up pissing and moaning about the dump."

The strip bars had long ago lost their allure for me. They certainly weren't erotic, although some of the women could be attractive. And it's not that I had a sudden attack of political correctness. My repeated explanation for my hesitation centered on boredom. I had to be engulfed with alcohol to enjoy the sight of mercenary women clumsily prancing to loud rock music while they cajoled tips from obnoxious, leering men.

He tossed me the keys to his car.

"Come on. You drive. I've been at it since this afternoon. We'll leave if it really gets to you."

And that settled it.

I returned the keys and had Felix follow me to my house,

where I parked the tank. Then I took over as chauffeur. I drove north on Federal Boulevard for about twenty blocks. The street was four lanes wide and traffic was heavy. Carpet warehouses, motorcycle shops, and flea markets rolled up to meet us and then drifted by as we snaked up and down the congested hills. The buildings were squat tin-covered garages with garish signs or cheap motels offering XXX-rated movies. Trailer homes lined up behind a giant wooden cowboy who straddled the side of the street, daring anyone to enter. The spirit of the Old West lived on.

The Honeypot fit in with the general atmosphere like a flat cigar at a bachelor party. I parked Gato's late-model Buick in the lot, locked all four doors, and then we walked through an entrance made up to look like a beehive. We paid five dollars each at the door and searched for seats in the brazen black-light glare of the strip joint.

We found space at Stage Three, a round platform bathed in blue and red lights that offered us Teri as we sat down. She was a tall, skinny brunette who gyrated to the sound of Bruce Springsteen and eventually stretched facedown on a sparkling rug. She wiggled her rear end, spread her legs, and lovingly patted her crotch. Her fingers rubbed her skin through a black G-string that allowed enough to show to guarantee nice tips but not enough for a bust by one of the undercover cops who prowled the bar waiting for that extra inch of forbidden flesh, that intimate caress from one of the customers that would close the place for a few weeks until the appropriate fines were paid.

"She's okay. A little close to the bone. Where've you been, Gato?"

I was referring to his vanishing act of the past several years, but he chose to ignore the real meaning of my question.

"Had to close up the store. Manny left early, his wife's birthday or something, so I stuck around. There wasn't

46

much happening. I wonder if Bruce knows what these ladies do to his music."

A waitress in red bikini shorts and a loose silky top took our orders for two beers.

I offered a comment on the talent. "You know, she looks like Becky—what was her name? The tall, thin, thin woman. Remember? She was with us that night we got chased out of the park by the cops' helicopter. The night that guy torched himself. Great night."

Felix nodded his head in agreement.

"Yeah, I remember. That long-haired kid had a Molotov, tried to throw it at the cops, but all he did was set his clothes on fire. He went running down the street, slapping at his shirt like a maniac."

Felix flailed at his back, blowing his breath at imaginary flames that leapt from his clothes. He acted out the wild scene for my benefit, although there was no doubt in either of our minds that I knew the story as well as he did.

" 'Fire, fire, I'm on fucking fire!' "

I couldn't help myself; ardent, nostalgia-induced laughter doubled me over as we remembered the boy with the ponytail flying behind him, flames flicking up from his back, chased by riot-squad policemen carrying long wooden clubs and wearing gas masks. Looking back, it was funny, but when it had happened, Felix, the girl, and yours truly were beaten and left in the park, the girl crying hysterically, the boys too roughened up to comfort her.

Teri finished her act and a woman named Cinnamon paraded across the stage, dancing to music that progressively hardened into just this side of white noise. She feigned enthusiasm as her discarded garments accumulated in small mounds, until only the G-string for the dollar bills remained on her lithe body.

I told Gato that we should leave. A short, very blond woman jumped on the stage. The announcer shouted over the speaker system, "And now, on Stage Three, the women just keep getting prettier, and younger! Presenting the very athletic, and sex-x-xy, Misty!" Her face had deep blue eyes. Her tanned flesh glistened. Large round breasts bounced beneath a shiny spandex T-shirt, the type worn by jogging women at City Park. Felix stared hard at the woman as she stripped down to red high heels and a red ribbony string.

A group of men in suits and ties stumbled to the stage, shouting, whistling—former fraternity brothers on a binge. The men hollered at the blonde, demanding that she dance only for them. They piled dollar bills at her feet and she favored them with as much attention as their money bought. One of the men produced a roll of toilet paper from inside his suit coat with a presentation that would have been envied by Houdini. He wrapped a makeshift turban around his head, then passed the roll to the other men. In seconds, they all had carelessly torn sheets of white tissue wrapped around their heads, across their ears, drooping across their foreheads. They laughed and shouted; it was New Year's Eve with paper hats, dancing women, and plenty of booze.

Felix and I tried to ignore them as they stood at the stage, clapping their hands in unison, shouting, "Take it off! Take it off! All the way off!" Misty grinned and rotated her body for the men, delighting them into screaming for more.

Felix shook his head and motioned with his beer bottle that we should move. We carried our drinks to the back of the bar and the appropriate isolation of a table where we could talk.

"It's been a long time, Louie. We don't get together like we used to. I miss those times."

"We're older, bud. Can't keep up. Got to survive. You know how it is."

He nodded without responding. He related to survival. Gato's business—Cuahtemoc Liquors—always seemed to be on the verge of going under. If he wasn't dealing with the tax man or city inspectors or the licensing board, then he had trouble with pilfering employees or the sunken economy or just plain bad timing. I was inured to his stories of impending disaster. The truth was that he had owned the store for only about a year and it was hardly an institution on the Northside. Yet, the red-and-blue neon sign of an Aztec warrior standing before smoking volcanoes, a torch in each hand, and the word CUAHTEMOC blinking interminably into the night from the store's huge barred front window added the right touch of culture to my neighborhood.

"Speaking about how it is, Felix. I had a bad time with one of your ex-relatives today—Ed Talmage, up in Central City. What is it with him? I mentioned your name and it was like opening the lid on his casket. You two don't get along?"

"You could say that, bro. The old man threatened to break me, ruin me, have me arrested, you name it. He never expected his daughter to marry a Chicano deadbeat veteran. The guy didn't speak to me after we got married, and the only connection he had with Martha was because of Adela. When they died, that finished any relationship we might ever have had."

I hadn't intended to bring up Felix's wife and daughter, but it made sense that they were an integral part of the story between Talmage and the Cat. I should have guessed that, and I regretted it immediately. Adela had died in front of her parents in a freak elevator accident. Six months later, Martha jumped from the top of the same building. That's when Felix finally flipped out. He wandered the country for five years, lost and out of touch.

"Does Talmage even know you're back in town? It's been about fourteen, fifteen months, right?"

"Yeah, something like that. He might know, but we don't exactly move in the same circles. And I'm sure he doesn't care. He accused me of ruining Martha's life. Blamed me

49

for the deaths of Adela and Martha. He had a stroke when Martha killed herself. Put himself in that wheelchair because he couldn't get over what she had done. But that's not what's happening now, Louie."

He turned his attention to his beer and tried to avoid my gaze. His green eyes were misty, foggy, and I hated myself for stirring up the ashes of his dead wife and daughter.

"What is happening now, Felix? What are you up to?"

He responded eagerly, quickly.

"I've got my business, finally something going after the five years I somehow lost. I don't need Talmage and all he stands for—his hatred, mindless grief, pitiful racism. Not now, especially since I've found someone who wants to help me start over."

Felix began his private tale of calamity and resurrection, the words coming out in a rush. I couldn't have been more surprised. He was not the talking kind. Whatever went on in his head was buried deep, and that's where he kept it. He came off as the guy with ultimate control, so cool and withdrawn that nothing fazed him, nothing got to him. I didn't know the person who had wandered the country, homeless and sick. I heard that he'd lost control then, and he never talked with me about what he did, where he went, or how he'd finally checked into a VA hospital and snapped out of it. The only Felix I knew was Gato, and whoever it was during those five lost years had been left behind, along with the tears and memories of his family.

But I had actually lived long enough finally to hear a hint of human vulnerability in the resonant voice of Felix Guerrero.

"I ran into her at one of those Hispanic Chamber of Commerce things where everybody slaps backs and trades numbers. What can I tell you, bro? You wouldn't like her. You're attracted by the cultural types, the dark *mestizas*, spouting Chicano poetry while they clean a pot of beans."

His description was dated—no self-respecting Chicana cleaned beans for any man these days—but I let him rattle on, intrigued by his newly acquired loquaciousness.

"Elizabeth's beautiful—that's the only word. We talked, and it was like I was a kid again. I don't know, man; have you ever just wanted to be next to a woman, not even touching her, just looking at her, taking it all in, sort of letting whatever it is creep under your skin?"

If I had, I wasn't going to tell him about it, not right then. This was a side of Felix I should have suspected existed, but it had never appeared in all the time we'd tramped together.

"I didn't try anything. I didn't push for us to start anything. It all just sort of happened, like it was supposed to, and it was more natural than I remembered, man."

I said the first thing that popped into my head.

"What's her racket, Felix, her angle?"

"*Qué* Louie, always looking for the *movida*. What happened to make you so cynical?"

"That's for another night. This Elizabeth, what does she do? If you don't mind me prying?"

"Louie, I'm the one that wanted to talk, remember? Whatever you want to know. She's an accountant, if you can believe that. She consults for different outfits, like that architect who's planning the mall on South Broadway."

I wrinkled my nose. The El Dorado Project had been splashed around for years and I thought it had died a deserved death when the bond financial package expired at the hands of a miserly, and wary, city council. It was impossible for me to believe that Gato would have fallen for anybody even remotely associated with upscale commercial development. *¿Y, además,* an accountant? All the number crunchers I had ever met were forgettable, unless an anal nature and the apparent ability to make even sex boring counted as remarkable traits.

"Of course, she does work for her husband, too."

51

My head must have jerked noticeably, because he quit talking for just enough of a pause to make us both feel awkward. Without looking at me, he continued.

"By the time I tried to get a grip on the fact that she was married, I was in so deep, I didn't really care."

A bell rang; an alarm shrieked; a whistle blew. If the bar hadn't been so warm, shivers would have run up and down my back. Gato's affair with a married woman required him to unburden himself on someone, and there I was. I knew then why he had called me after weeks of not even bothering to check the obituaries for my name. My record with women was spotty, to say the least, and he had to suspect that if any of his aging buddies had experience with this sort of thing, Luis Montez, Esq., was the most likely candidate.

The screech level in the Honeypot turned up about a hundred notches on the decibel meter. All the girls lined up on the stages for a group grope dance. Men stood in the aisles and on chairs, clapping, yelling, almost unwilling to believe that ten nearly naked women were bunched together, rubbing against one another, squirming, warming up for the big show when they paraded through the bar, giving the customers cheap thrills while the announcer begged and pleaded for the men to buy shots of overpriced alcohol to toast the lovely display of well-toned flesh.

I shouted through the din.

"I told you this place was bad news. Never again, Felix. I've had it with this nonsense."

He shrugged his shoulders.

"Maybe you're right. Let's go."

We escaped before the mad dance ignited whatever remained of the crowd's inhibitions.

6

_A_s I drove, he talked about the wonderful Elizabeth. My attention was split between him and my time with Sylvia. Felix had been right. I had firsthand experience with such complications.

Does anyone who gets caught up in these things realize that the sex is so damn good only because it's forbidden? We'd had the greatest time two people can have in bed, or in the backseat of a car, or under a blanket on a mountainside. The reason for the affair is never important. There is no explanation for how it started, nothing that makes sense, anyway. Back then, I was still married to Dolores, my second wife, and although it was clear to everyone except her mother that we had run our course, I honestly was not looking for a replacement. And Sylvia also was married, but she wasn't at the end of anything, at least not before she hooked up with me.

Driving through the thickening night, with Gato's lament the only sound in the car, I compared his current anguish with my own of several years ago, and the memories tugged at me as much as on the day they were created. I obsessed about feelings I thought I had buried with the time-honored ceremonies of drinking and indiscriminate womanizing. Haphazard, out-of-sequence thoughts bumped themselves out of my head when he dredged up that old romantic pain: the softness of the crook of Sylvia's elbow, where my hand fell automatically when we walked together; scratches on her legs from romps with her dog; her tongue caressing my lower lip.

I would lie with her in a motel, a cheap TV popping and snapping in the background, both of us naked, uncovered and unashamed. My arms wrapped around her in automatic gestures meant to signify her importance to me. My hunger was overwhelming. I was crazy for her and told her so and she said she would do anything for me so many times that I lost count, and the sad part was that we believed each other.

She stared at me with heavy eyes in those moments, the lust a tangible third party in the bed, groaning and grunting with us, whispering lewd noises and words in our ears that made sweat glisten on our skin while tender fingers gently caressed us to that point where the light in the room merged into a thin white line of desire and that's all we knew.

Felix blubbered on and I tried to pay attention. It was an old story with a great mix of romance, guilt, tenderness, and sneaking away for quick love in the afternoon. They had finally stopped only because Elizabeth was afraid that something would arouse her husband's suspicions, such as her abandonment of marital sex, or maybe the strange hours her work suddenly demanded.

"I can't confront not seeing her, Louie. She's in my head constantly—a buzz in my brain that I can't shake, a feeling I can't turn off when I think about her with her husband, when I think about what she would tell me, how she made me feel. I'm fucked up, Louie."

I told him to quit wasting my time. I didn't want to be

part of the seamy back-door entanglement that I knew without a doubt couldn't have a happy ending.

"It's Pandora's box, Felix. No matter what you tell each other, once you open it, you can't get back to where you were when you started. Someone's going to get hurt, and it's always the innocent who hurt the most. Think of the other guy."

"I have, Louie. Trini Anglin hasn't been innocent since he was about seven years old."

It was that kind of year.

The words flowed from his mouth as if they were butter melting on a hot tortilla. For an instant, I refused to believe Felix had uttered that name.

"You remember, Elizabeth married him while they were still up at the university."

I mechanically slapped the steering wheel. Elizabeth, Beticia—one and the same. A girl we had known when we were still on the streets, a girl who worked her way out of the barrio by marrying into an established and venerable Northside organization.

The Anglin family story was well known to anybody from the Northside. I had heard it ever since I was a kid watching the Anglin Cadillacs and Mercedes drive by my partners and me as we loitered along Thirty-eighth. The story continued through the years and I heard it in bits and pieces, at the courthouse, from cops and other lawyers, or read it in the newspapers. Vincent Anglin, the head of the clan, had connections to more than a dozen successful businesses—restaurants, flower shops, dry cleaners, floating crap games, crack houses, and prostitution rings. And dear Elizabeth had married Trini, the third and only surviving son of Vincent's infamous marriage to Nita Alvarez, another woman who understood the power of an appropriate spouse within the intricate machinations of Northside ambition.

The Anglins were Denver's authentic crime family, and Elizabeth was the wife of the crown prince.

As kids, Felix and I and every young dude for twenty blocks wanted to make out with *la Betty* because she had the sweetest-looking lips of all the girls who hung around the gym after the football dances or gathered in sultry groups in the backyards of summer parties. It had been years since I had talked with her, although periodically her still-seductive mouth sulked at me across my morning coffee from the society pages of the newspaper.

There is no dealing with a fool in love, and if that fool happens to be Chicano, *ya 'stuvo.*

"I'm not going to be very sympathetic, Felix. Only an idiot would mess around with Trini Anglin's wife, even if she is an old squeeze. If he finds out . . ."

"He has."

I forgot about driving, about maintaining so we wouldn't draw any undue attention from the police patrolling Federal for late-night drunks. Damn, I forgot about waking up the next morning. If Trini Anglin knew about Elizabeth and Felix we both could be incinerated in an explosion any minute, and our noisy departures would hardly rate three lines in the obituaries.

"Cause of death—stupidity."

Finally, at four in the morning, Felix quit talking and my glow-in-the-dark digital told me it was time to go. I sat on his sagging overstuffed sofa, drinking one beer after another, regretting that it was one of those nights when the alcohol had no effect. I guess he did most of the talking. I remember almost constantly shaking my head in pity or anger. No matter what I said, it wouldn't help Felix. My affair with Sylvia had turned into one of the all-time bad scenes, without any exhortative lessons for me to pass on to my bewitched buddy.

A baggy brown vinyl easy chair huddled in the corner. A

few books took up space in the shelves next to the fireplace. On one wall hung Adela's crayon drawing of a storm over a bridge, which she had given him as a memento of a visit to San Francisco. Another wall held his framed poster of Emiliano Zapata. The Mexican guerrilla leader stood tall and straight, proud, dressed to the nines in his *charro* outfit, holding a shiny Winchester with a leather thong on the stock. Sad-eyed *peón* prophet, still handsome after all these years.

In contrast to Zapata, and directly across from him, Martha and Adela smiled at the room from the same picture I had seen the day before in Talmage's office. Felix had carelessly leaned it on his fireplace mantel. He had ordered the portrait for their twelfth anniversary party, the last one they celebrated before Martha died.

He agitated himself into a raucous drunk as he spewed out wild tales of mad love with Elizabeth on the run, secret meeting places, clever telephone codes, and mind-burning paranoia. I hoped he hadn't lost it completely.

I tried to come across as wise rather than as a wiseass, but talking with Felix always had been an exercise in understatement and indirectness. If I had to describe our method of communicating, it would have to be beating around the bush.

"I've never told you Felix, because there wasn't any reason to, but I was having an affair at the time Dolores was divorcing me. So maybe it wasn't technically an affair, for me."

"Was the woman alone?"

"That's the bad part, man. She was married, and our thing together screwed up her life, and mine for a while, too. Even though we talked about not falling in love, about not hurting innocent people, about not getting so involved that we couldn't step back when we wanted to and cut it loose—it all went to pieces one day."

Felix slumped back in his chair and listened to me the

best he could. I hoped he was coherent enough to listen and that I was smart enough to make sense. The odds weren't good on either one of those propositions.

"What happened?"

"We got busted, what else? Her husband found us together in an embarrassing situation, so to speak. There was a hideous spectacle that got real close to violence. That whole scene still stirs up my stomach and makes my hands shake. She and her husband moved away."

"You never saw her again? No calls, nothing?"

"Once. The day before they moved. Wanted to close things out, she said. It was bad, Felix. Very bad. I'm sure she'd been going through hell. She looked like it—worn-out, uptight. All I could think about was that it wasn't worth it, man. There was no reason for me to inflict that much pain on anyone, all in the name of love or sex or whatever."

"She blamed you?"

"The funny thing is, she didn't. She knew exactly what she was getting into, she said. She told me she still cared for me. She still thought that if things had played out differently, we could have had a good life together. But in the end, she had to try to make it work with her old man, and I had to give her the chance to do that. So she said."

"In other words, stay away."

"I haven't seen or heard from her since. I got physically sick from that episode, Felix. That buzz you mentioned—it was a roar for me. I thought the earth revolved around my pitiful experience with lost love and frustrated lust. My drinking really got to be a problem. My practice was a disaster. I took it out on Dolores, Gloria, the kids, my old man—everybody. They thought it was because of the divorce, but I was so screwed up over Sylvia that everything else seemed small and unimportant. It's just not worth it, Felix."

58

I wasn't getting through. A sadder-than-usual grimace graced his face as he sipped on an almost-empty beer.

"What Elizabeth and I have . . . it's not like you and—what's her name?"

"Sylvia."

"Sylvia. We didn't lie to ourselves about not getting so heavy with each other that we could lose perspective. We lost that from the jump. I guess I just don't give a damn what the consequences are, bud. It's been a long time since I had anyone, since I cared about a person. I found that again with Elizabeth, and I'm not going to lose it. I couldn't take it, not again. It's happening, and right now I can't think of a way to stop it, nor do I want to."

There's only one response for that kind of talk.

"Pendejo."

Maybe scare tactics would work, since reason and logic didn't appear to matter.

"And then you go and pick up on a wise guy's woman. I thought you were smarter than that. Trini knows you, man. He remembers us from the days when we were all kids. You're on the lip here. And you better get it together before Anglin's boys take you for one of those famous rides on Lookout Mountain. People who mess with Anglin, or Anglin's things, turn up with their brains splattered all over Jefferson County. Come on, man! She can't be that good!"

He stood up. He stared at me for a second, then tossed his beer with a heave stronger than necessary. The beer smashed into the garbage can, sending it spinning across the floor. He muttered one word. "Fuck." Then he sat back down. It was my turn to stare at him.

"Look. I can't talk to you about how I feel about Elizabeth. You can't ever know the way we feel. But there are a couple of things. Maybe then you won't think I'm the devil or something like that."

I stayed with my hard face and didn't respond.

"Elizabeth has been trying to leave Anglin for years. Everything you ever heard about the guy is true. He's made her life a nightmare. He beats her up, treats her like shit. He's had other women ever since they were married. Damn, she knows that he screwed one of the bridesmaids in a car in the parking lot outside their wedding reception! She was in love with him, but he managed to kill that."

I felt I should say the apparent truth.

"Felix, there is such a thing as divorce, and plenty of divorce lawyers. This isn't the Dark Ages, when a woman has to stay with a man till death do them part."

"Sure, sure. That's easy to say. I even said that's what she had to do. And she tried, man. She would leave his ass, then go back. Then something else would happen, another fight, she would leave, then he would beg her to come back. The way she talked, it happened over and over and over. It was a mix of her own guilt and self-blame and his pathetic begging. I guess he can be fairly charming, in a snake kind of way. It's like she was trapped. For a long time, she thought she couldn't control what was going on."

I knew the scenario. I had heard it a hundred times from my divorce clients, who somehow existed in the abuse cycle for years. Sometimes even a divorce decree didn't stop it.

"There was one time, before I met her. She finally reached her breaking point. He had her brother's arm broken because of bets he was late on paying up. She confronted him about it, and he laughed in her face. He called her a stupid Mexican, if you can believe that, and screamed and hollered about all of her lazy relatives. He threatened her and her family. He said she could never leave unless she rode out in a hearse. But she worked up enough courage so that finally she wasn't afraid of him. She told him she was getting out, no matter what he did, and he went berserk. After that little confrontation, she had to leave town for three weeks, just so she could avoid her family. She didn't want to scare her mother. She was afraid somebody might see the bruises."

We sat in silence. There wasn't anything for me to say, and Felix had talked himself into a semiconscious state. Eventually, long after his dime-store cuckoo crowed out the half hour, he said something I wasn't sure was meant for me.

"She doesn't know what to do."

When he passed out, I switched off the lights and made sure his door was locked. He lived in a rough part of the neighborhood.

7

_____◆_____

I sacked out for three hours, then crawled through a shower. Two nights with Felix meant two mornings-after suffering from too little sleep and too much jagged energy. I struggled to stay alert on the drive to my office. I had forgotten about my bruised eye until the throb on the right side of my face stirred up effulgent memories of the Capri. Groggy and punch-drunk, I stopped at a diner for coffee. The place looked as bad as I felt, and I was only pretending to be a functioning human being.

A waitress poured me cup after cup of coffee, but it didn't seem to help. I wasn't even sure of the name of the joint.

For several weeks, the air had been clear and warm. During the long night with Felix, the weather had relapsed and the day started gray and windy, with moisture hanging in the sky, a sign that the miserable winter still clung desperately to its icy existence. It was a perfect cover for my mood. The people around me moved to the beat of a crippled strobe. They were hazy, incomplete figures.

A couple walked in. The woman was bundled up in scarves, earmuffs, a stocking cap, a frayed black coat, and moon boots. The man wore only a shiny pair of slacks, gym shoes, an orange sweatshirt, and a blue piece of cloth wrapped around his neck. They sat in the booth near the back wall. I could hear every word they mumbled to each other.

The man said, "I only got enough for coffee. You want coffee, don't you, honey?"

"Yeah, sure. Coffee, whatever."

The waitress filled my cup and left the bill. She then turned her attention to the couple. She waited for them to order.

Frank read over the menu, studied it.

"Say, is this the Casita or Don Juan's or what? Everything changes, always changing. Sheesh, can't keep up sometimes. Two coffees, senior-eeta. Two coffees."

After the waitress left, Frank whispered to Joan, "Need to speak Spanish to get through to these people."

"Right, Frank, I keep forgettin' you're bilingual."

"Damn, I only got a buck twenty, enough for coffee. I hope."

Joan wanted to talk about profound matters.

"I can't believe Barbara, not letting you in like that."

"Hey, my own sister, and she won't give me my check—Christ, not until Thursday—but she don't say how we're supposed to eat until then. So for now I got a buck twenty." The waitress placed two cups in front of Frank and Joan. "Coffee's hot, anyway. Say, baby, you got any money?"

"Frank, I told you, I ain't got a cent; you know that. Quit askin'."

"Hey, hey, that's okay by me. You get half my check, whenever your boyfriend the mailman delivers it, and I get half yours. Share and share alike, peas in a pod. We both eat. We manage to catch a ride up to Central City, hit the jackpot and blow this hole. One of these days."

He chuckled over the thought of finally getting rich off the slot machines in the mountains.

Joan grumbled. "You're an old fool, Frank, you know that?"

"Okay, okay, I get it. I talk too much; you don't have to say it. I go on and on, yeah sure. We ought to go, pay the bill, get out of here. I got a dollar twenty. If the coffee is a buck, I still got twenty cents to call Barbara, but then I can't leave a tip. You sure you ain't got no money? How much coffee can we get for a buck? Maybe a warmer?"

The waitress poured more coffee for the couple. Frank and I had drunk enough coffee to float Colombia.

"You sure you don't want something to eat?"

"No, no, I ate at the Center, like you should've. What are you doing with that beard? Why can't you shave? You look like a convict, for God sakes."

"It ain't like I got a goddamn maid comes around and pinches my cheeks until I get up, is it? It ain't like I got my own butler to lather up my face and shave off my whiskers, is it? I'll shave at one, when we go back to the place. Don't worry about it. Then I'll call Barbara, if that damn Leonard will let me talk to her. He bawled me out all the way over there and all the way back, and they didn't even let me in the damn house. Wouldn't give me my check. Sheesh, treat me like a kid, my own sister."

Joan patted his hands.

"Take it easy, Frank. You'll have another attack. I couldn't stomach that right now."

"Oh yeah! Like last night, two nights ago, whooee! I was out of it then, out in left field."

"You were zonkers. You worry me when you get like that."

"That was bad, man, bad. Strapped down at Denver General, last night, two nights ago. They had to keep me there all night, at least all night. Sheesh, what a night."

Joan eyed the waitress standing near the cash register, who was doing her own staring at Frank.

"Let's get out of here. They ain't gonna give us any more coffee."

"Yeah, I better pay the check. Here, I got a buck twenty, just enough for the coffee and a phone call. Say, baby, you got any money?"

I trudged behind the odd couple. The waitress took my money and smiled as she asked me to return. I answered, "Sure, sure," but I knew I wouldn't find the place again.

The man and woman stood outside the door, standing in the spring wind. The temperature had refused to climb since dawn and the accumulating clouds were a sure sign of a wild shower, maybe a hailstorm or even a tornado.

Joan tightened the blue rag around Frank's neck and then pulled her cap over her earmuffs. She placed her hand in Frank's as they walked off, talking about checks and bitchy sisters and good hot coffee.

I stared at my ragged pocket calendar and didn't see anything that would force me to go to the office. I would miss calls for new business, and I had to return a slew of messages before they turned as stale as last week's shirt, but with my numb brain and sore eye, I couldn't face up to sitting around my desk. Felix's mess stuck to me overnight. Concentration on anything as trivial as my economic survival was out of the question. The strongest coffee in town waited in an ever-present pot at my father's house. It seemed like the right time.

Jesús Genaro Montez greeted me with a grunt. He was sweeping his front walk with a broom almost as hairless as the top of his head. His fedora, askew and balanced delicately on the back of his neck, moved with each turn of the broom and shook in the chilly wind.

"Well, look what the cat drug in. What have you been up to? ¿Y tu ojo? How can you focus out of that thing?"

"It's always a pleasure to see you, too, Dad. Got any coffee?"

He led me inside and poured two cups of coffee that he had to cut with a knife. I added plenty of milk. With my first drink, I felt a surge of energy along my spine, straight to my brain and eventually into my black eye. Instant headache.

"Jesus, Jesús. What's in this mess?"

I rubbed my forehead and managed to move the pain to the center of my head.

"Don't drink it, son, if you can't take it. Your mother and me worked out the recipe for perfect coffee when you were still waving your pee-pee in everybody's face and laughing when you wet all over yourself. It's the best damn coffee you'll ever drink."

"Dad, you do it differently every time you make a pot. I've seen you. One day you throw in an eggshell; the next day you add cinnamon; another day, just for grins, you put in a tea bag or spoonful of chocolate. I'm surprised you haven't poisoned yourself."

"It's a secret recipe, Louie. If I see anybody watching me, including nosy lawyers like you, then I'm liable to do anything to keep it secret. But like I said, if you can't take it, don't drink it. If you can't stand the heat, don't ask for the treat."

He shook his finger at me and bopped his head to a tune only he could hear. A seventy-year-old rapper. My father had finally gone over the big cliff we all face at the end of the road.

"Have the boys been by to visit? The last time I saw them, they promised."

"Yeah, sure. Good kids. I see them more than you. Their mother, too. She stopped by and had a cup of coffee. Thought it was delicious."

Gloria always had been a favorite of Dad's. She knew how to cultivate their relationship.

"Good, I'm glad to hear that. They don't like to visit me,

I'll tell you that. They think they're too old for their father anymore."

"I wonder where they got that?"

He clucked his teeth and turned on the radio. A solid Mexican love song blared out and I had to turn it down a bit. We drank coffee and listened to the young female voice pour out the story of her lost love, the trumpets lifting her words across the room, the sadness matching exactly the weather, my mood, and the pain in my eye.

"You remember Felix Guerrero, Dad? One of the guys from high school. I brought him by a year ago or so."

"Sure. *Veterano,¿no?* Nice guy. A gentleman. I wondered how you knew him."

"He used to come by the house when we were kids. Everybody called him Felix the Cat, Gato."

"His eyes, no doubt."

"That, and just the way he took care of himself—always in control, real independent. He would disappear for days and then show up like nothing had happened. The rest of us didn't worry. We were jealous. But he didn't have much of a family life. Now that I think about it, I'm surprised he didn't end up in Cañon City, one of my clients. But he turned out all right."

He responded in Spanish. *"Well, you shouldn't be surprised. So many people nowadays . . . I don't get it. They expect the worst out of people. It should be the other way around. We should be surprised when a kid goes bad; we shouldn't accept it. We shouldn't think somebody was lucky because he stayed straight."*

He took a very healthy drink of coffee just in case he wanted to get wound up. My father had mellowed. When I was a kid, I thought he was a terror, a man who taught with fear, control, and, so he said, example. After my mother died, he went through a period when he resented youth. He castigated all kids and pretended to be caught up in the antiadolescent paranoia that many of his friends

67

harped on at the bingo parlors. But the past few years had changed him. His relationship with Bernardo and Eric had deepened into a closeness that he had never shared with his own children, and his new attitude carried over into improved contacts with the children of my brothers and sisters when they were in town. In a quirky twist, it was I who now harbored the jaundiced view of the teenage world.

He continued his lecture. "That's the way it's supposed to happen. I see the kids around here—most of them are good. They just need a little attention. They're going to be okay if nobody screws around with them."

His eyes traveled over the potted plants in his window and out to the group of young boys loitering on the corner.

"But I also know that some of them are monsters, Louie. Created by their parents or the schools or the way they have to live, or maybe they're just bad. *¿Quién sabe?* But it's no different now than when I was a kid, or you were. I think we all just know about it more."

I didn't agree with him, but I didn't argue. It wouldn't have done any good. As far as I was concerned, the children of America were almost a lost cause. I saw too many cruel and hardened criminals in the juvenile courts not to think otherwise. They paraded through the courthouse shackled together, laughing and joking, some on the first step of a long journey into prison life. All colors and sizes—their only common denominator was that they were not old enough to vote.

"That may be, Dad. At least Felix is a solid citizen. He has his own business; he did his bit in the war. He was dealt a couple of dirty hands—Vietnam, his daughter's accident. And then he lost his wife. That about killed him. His mind snapped. He turned into one of those guys waiting for sandwiches at the mission. But he bounced out of it and overcame."

My father squinted over his cup.

"The daughter's death, and then the wife, all in one year. If that had happened to me, I don't know how I would have kept on. The worst thing that ever happened to me was your mother's passing. I cried like a child, and we had been together for thirty years. Felix is either very tough or so scarred that the pain sits under his skin, waiting to pour out. No man deserves what he went through."

"Yet, he's the same guy I remember, who could move through any situation. Always was cool."

I paused, swirled the coffee in my cup, and made my point.

"Until now. He's lost his bearings."

"Must be a woman. *Como siempre.*"

"You're good, Dad."

He cracked a smile underneath the shaggy and gray remnants of a fifty-year-old mustache.

I described the affair and asked him what he thought. He acted as if he didn't have an opinion.

"It's his neck. If he was here and he asked me, I might tell him to turn it loose. At least think it over. Let the lady end what she got into first and then he can be as romantic as he wants." He turned off the Spanish.

"He wouldn't listen. Every cool guy I ever knew eventually got tripped up by a woman, including me. Some like it and go with it and some can't handle it and make a mess out of everything. I think Felix is the kind who can handle it . . . *pero, ¿quién sabe?*"

"Her husband's a gangster, Dad. Doesn't that mean anything?"

"The husband is always something, Louie. It may be a little more exciting because of Anglin's reputation, but messing around can be dangerous even if the other guy delivers pizzas."

The coffee and the talk had done the job. I actually thought I could do a little work. I promised to drop by again, later in the week, and I also promised to call the kids.

He went back to cleaning up the front of his house. One of the neighbor's young sons strolled over, and I watched from my car, just in case. The kid swaggered, his hands stuffed in his pockets and a shit-eating grin plastered across his zit-scarred face. His pants drooped around his knees and his eyes shined a bit too brightly for my comfort level. My father handed him the broom and the two divided chores. It was apparent they had worked together previously.

8

———————◆———————

*T*he rest of that day was long and tiring. A blurry con-
glomeration of paperwork, phone calls, client interviews,
dictation, phone calls, paperwork, phone calls. Near the
end, I finished one call and then, before I hung up,
punched in the number of my reluctant client. Why not?
The phone was warm.

Jenny agreed to meet in a park near her house.

"Too crazy at my place," she explained.

A late-afternoon shower moved gently through the city.
Unlike the earlier wind, the storm brought warm rain and
the illusion of summer. A silver curtain of water washed
through the end of day blues and turned a few of the city's
frustrations into targets for "always tomorrow." By the
time I arrived at Columbus Park, thunder and lightning
played tag across the horizon and an iron-colored pall
hung in the air, but the rain had stopped, leaving dripping
trees and wet benches in the park. A rainbow arched over
the downtown skyline, twisting among the skyscrapers,
bouncing rays of color off the chrome and glass.

I found my client sitting on a damp newspaper spread
across a defaced picnic table, smoking a cigarette. She

saw me coming and stamped out her smoke. She offered a handshake and a "How are you counselor?" She stared at my shiner and smiled to herself but didn't mention it. I was grateful for that.

This urban Chicana certainly tried to fit the role a surly destiny had created for her. She wore ripped sneakers, splotched blue jeans, and a black sleeveless T-shirt with red and green lettering that advertised DR. LOCO'S ROCKIN' JALAPEÑO BAND. Petite and chunky, she could have been the inspiration for Dr. Loco's song about his *"linda cholita."* Black hair, just this side of spiked, and an attractive face were set off by muscular arms. The initials D.V. were tattooed across her left shoulder. She had five kids, no long-term man, and a reputation as a hell-raising, grassroots woman who had occasionally managed to move the forces that controlled her part of the barrio. I knew she had taken on greedy councilmen, corrupt cops, perverted priests, and lazy teachers. I also knew she had slowed down in the last few years. Evangelina told me that was because of Victor, her eldest, who had created his own reputation in the community. Victor Rodríguez, almost seventeen, had been described by Evangelina as a "mean and vicious gang-banger." What sin had Jenny passed on to her son?

I also knew that times were hard for Jenny and her family. The Northside had suffered the brunt of the economic decline in the city the past few years. Jenny had grown up in the projects, found work where she could, had seen two of her brothers die violently in the streets, and still waited for a third listed as missing in action. Yet she always managed to persevere. For several years, she had worked in a factory near Globeville pasting together unpainted furniture. It wasn't glamorous or challenging, but it paid more than the minimum wage, and eventually she'd become a line supervisor. It was a blow to the entire neighborhood when the place closed down and laid off its hundred workers. Jenny hadn't found any replacement employment in more than a year.

I knew the lawsuit could help her and her kids. Quitting didn't make any sense.

"Tell me it isn't so, Jenny, and we can end this quickly and I'll buy you a cup of coffee." My father's special brew had worn off.

"I'm sorry, Louie, but I got to call it. It ain't worth it. What's it going to mean, anyway? After I go through all this court stuff—depositions and hearings and examinations by their doctors and the trial and whatever else you legal eagles can come up with—then what? The cops won't ever beat up anybody else again? I can feel safe having a drink, without worrying about getting jumped by some fat honky with a need to punch out Chicanas? It just ain't fucking worth it."

She lit another cigarette.

"Come on, Jenny, you knew all that before we started. I explained all this, outlined the steps. And *you* told me that it wouldn't matter in the long run but that you had to do something. They hurt you, Jenny—bad. Don't let them get away with it."

She looked at me through a puff of smoke and I realized this wasn't about her. Jenny had been through worse. She was a fighter, not a quitter. She could overcome all the legal rigmarole, and she could endure all the poking and probing by city lawyers and doctors. All she really wanted was a chance to stand up and tell the world what had happened, and for that chance she was willing to go through as much grief as the bureaucrats and their hacks wanted to dump on her. The thing that could make her change had to be connected to someone else, someone she cared for more than herself.

"How's Victor?"

"Shit."

73

She flicked the cigarette in the general direction of the mountains.

"Leave it, counselor. It's my case and I'm telling you to end it. If that's not done, then . . ."

I grabbed her arm, but she jerked away. She stared me down.

"What, Jenny? If the case doesn't end, then what?"

"Then you're fired."

She left gray footprints in the soggy grass.

I couldn't think of anything except to talk with Evangelina and try to persuade her to help keep Jenny in the ball game.

I had noticed the group of boys when I parked my car, but I didn't think too much about them. Columbus Park was in the heart of the Northside and there was always plenty of *gente* milling around its shady environs or the immediate blocks that surrounded it. Years ago, the people who hung out in the park had renamed it La Raza Park. The city fathers, of course, had refused to officially recognize the renaming.

The guy in the leather baseball cap somehow was directly in front of me. I glanced at him with a look that I hoped said, I don't have time for anything, dude, so excuse me and I'll just be on my way. Maybe that was too much to expect from one glance.

"What's the hurry, Homes?"

I swerved to get around him and that's when I finally saw the rest of the story. I stared at eight or nine black leather baseball caps sitting on half-shaved heads and foot-long rattails. Eight or nine left ears had three golden rings hanging from their lobes. I was surrounded by boys heavy into the Colorado Rockies. They all wore black-and-purple-hooded sweatshirts with black four-inch letters— CR—outlined in silver. The same logo repeated on the caps. Either this was the Rockies Northside youth project or I

74

had almost run over one of the Chicano Rocker Boys—the CRB. Rockies, all right, with a twist.

The CRB had roamed the streets for years. Originally, the gang called itself the Cool Rockers or the Chicano Rockers, depending on who made up the fluid membership at any particular time. This was long before the new baseball team had sparked a gleam in the mayor's eye. The Rockers eventually became the Rocker Boys, then the CRB, and it was only natural that the official birth of the Colorado Rockies also signaled the gang's wholesale adoption of the team's paraphernalia. The delinquent clotheshorses still roamed the street, as they did in the days when their gang really had been a social club, a crutch for poor kids without much else to lean on, but now their roaming had taken on an ugly edge. Crack, automatic weapons, and constant warfare with rivals added up to a schizoid lifestyle that often erupted into violence against one another and anyone else unlucky enough to wander into their playground.

"I know you can't be in that much of a hurry, lawyer. You almost ran into my homeboy Petey, and that would be a big mistake."

The kid doing the talking was a little shorter than the rest of the squad, but the way he directed their movements left no doubt that he was the leader. His hands moved in tricky gestures and signs that I didn't have a clue about, but in the few seconds it took to get my bearings, the CRBs had closed in and isolated me from the world.

"You guys must have made a mistake. I don't . . ."

The leader stopped me by moving to within an inch of my face. A thin, limp mustache covered his upper lip and pimples flared around his nose. I smelled teenage sweat and marijuana breath.

"Cool it, lawyer. If Petey jumps, you get landed on, and I really don't feel that way about you—not yet, you know? I connect that lawyers like to talk, but this is *my* office, and I think you should just listen. *¿Entiendes?*"

I decided on my own that he didn't actually want an answer.

"My old lady says you were trying to help her out, so I guess that means me and my posse cut you a break. But now she wants this thing with the pigs to stop. You wouldn't be punk enough to fuck around with what she wants, would you?"

Victor weaved and his eyelids flickered. His high occasionally grabbed him and spun him around the universe, but I tried to be patient and waited for him to spit it all out.

"I just want to make sure you understand that the CRB also wants you to cool it. No more hassles for my old lady. You wrap it up so you're off the hook, everybody's happy. You got that, don't you?"

Darkness crept into the park and shielded our tête-à-tête from the street.

From Victor's side, Petey whispered.

"We're steady rockers, cool rockers, don't you forget it. We rock steady, play heady, make you regret it!"

The rap poem ingrained in Petey's brain must have been repeated a hundred times a day.

My patience came to a screeching halt. I wanted to do some rapping of my own with the teenage mutants, but then the CRB reception abruptly ended. More finger signs and some unintelligible grunts from Victor, Petey stepped back, the rest of the crew took off to different parts of the park, and I was free to climb into my car.

Victor weaved almost out of control, and for some reason, that made Petey smile. I drove away from the image of Victor leaning on the taller boy, about ready to fall off the earth, and Petey grinning as if he was an undertaker at an execution.

9

⸻◆⸻

We need help, Louie."

The words met me at my front door, taut and whispered in the darkness, but I would always recognize Felix's deep, slow voice. I unlocked the door and a short shadow slipped in ahead of me. A hint of expensive, subtle perfume floated into the room with the shadow. Felix followed into the foyer of my house, where the moonlight covered us like a beacon. I didn't feel particularly safe.

I watched as Felix and Elizabeth reached for each other, then turned to me. Wherever they were coming from, she had left in a hurry. A torn blue windbreaker clashed with a business skirt, while a flamboyant silky scarf scarcely protected her neck from the drizzle. The perfume must have come from the scarf. The moon picked up her face and accented her high cheekbones, and for an instant I envied the Cat. Then I remembered Trini Anglin.

The pout of her lips, and the careless dimples were just as I remembered from my adolescent fantasies when I watched her from the anonymity of a group of horny boys or caught her eye as she rode by in a car full of cruising girls, looking for the guy I apparently wasn't. Pachuco rock and doo-wop, the Wiggle-Wobble, Rockybilt burgers, and quarts of cheap beer and wine swirled together into a movie about teenage angst, or was it lust?

In self-defense, I quickly walked away and made a show of throwing my coat on the back of a chair. I looked out the window for strange cars and saw at least four. I shut the drapes, switched on my reading lamp, and we all sat around the littered dining room table.

Felix filled me in, his voice scratchy and dry while he held on to Elizabeth's hands.

"Crap hit first thing this morning. An inspector from the building department came by the store and cited me for a dozen bullshit so-called violations of the building code. Ridiculous stuff like illegal wiring, wrong-size doorways, improper temperatures in the cooler, blah-blah."

He threw a handful of formal-looking papers onto the stacks of bills, magazines, and newspapers strewn across my table. I looked at a few. They were insignificant items that usually were fixed up on the spot whenever an inspector thought they were worth mentioning. Lumped together, however, they could add up to one long headache for a small businessman operating on a short margin.

Felix continued. "I was going to call you to get these thrown out, challenge them before I get fined or shut down, or my license erased. Trini yanked a chain downtown and I get squeezed by a two-bit bureaucrat who's sucking on his chi-chi."

The Cat was fired up. He had this quirk about people leaving him alone—must have been a Chicano thing. Now he had to deal with very serious interference.

"Anglin had Elizabeth followed from her job. She met me at Southwest Plaza, in a restaurant we've used before. We were only having lunch, for Christ sake! It's a place he wouldn't go to in a hundred fucking years. No need for Anglin to go out that far just to get something to eat. But Joey Cuginello strolled into the joint, walked around, and made sure we saw him. He must've followed her, or we just ran out of luck."

We all knew they had used up their quota of luck the first time they managed to hide themselves from Anglin. They had been living on gravy for several weeks. I waited for an explanation about what I was supposed to do about this not entirely unexpected development.

Joey Cugie was Anglin's vice president in charge of public relations—he kept the public out of the outfit's business. Trini should have delegated his wife's affair to a close and trusted friend, but he didn't know anybody like that, so he had to rely on his closest and most ruthless associate.

"We didn't panic. I told Elizabeth to meet me here. It seemed safer than my house. You don't mind, do you, Louie?"

One of those questions without an answer.

"She can't go home, of course. We left separately. We've been waiting for you for a couple of hours."

My mouth had a difficult time forming words. I was incredibly thirsty.

"I'm not sure there's much I can do, unless you want me to file the divorce."

Elizabeth finally stirred. An ironic smile creased the lips that launched a thousand teenage erections. In the insufficient glare of my sixty-watt table lamp, I noticed a line of tan freckles across the bridge of her nose, barely visible against the tawny shading of her skin.

She was almost shouting. "Divorce? Trini will never go along with that—I don't care who my lawyer is. I think our real problem is figuring out how Felix stays alive and I stay free of that son of a bitch!"

I had to agree.

Felix made noises as if he was about to give us the idea we had been waiting for, but it looked like a stall to me. He was in so deep, he had to be useless in the idea category.

"We leave town, Elizabeth. We've known it's the only thing we can do. You're not safe anywhere around that guy. We take off and start over someplace else."

Her hand reached out and rubbed his ear. She pulled him close to her and kissed his forehead.

"You really are something, Felix. Where can we go? What can we do? You've got your business here, your friends, everything—your whole life. We knew this was a mistake when it started, and now it's all come down on top of you."

She stared at my wall clock while she talked, and I think I saw a tear or two slip down her cheek, but her voice held quiet and steady.

Felix held her hand to his lips and spoke to her knuckles.

"I love you. That's enough for me. I can get another store, protect you. I don't have a life here or anywhere else without you. Whatever we thought when we started doesn't matter anymore. All I know is you. And if Trini doesn't leave us alone—"

I thought I should interrupt. Felix obviously was not thinking clearly. The ex-marine had it in him to take care of his business one-on-one with Anglin. He understood violence, guns, and death in ways he had only hinted at through the years. I couldn't let it get that far. Gato's friend had to come through for him with at least a bow to reality.

"Look, you two. You have to protect yourselves, then plan what you have to do. There's a way to work this without any craziness. But if you don't come up with something, Anglin will make all the decisions for you."

That was someone's cue. A parade of bullets shattered my front window and sprayed my house, exploding chunks of wall and floor and cutting into the table and chairs that we knocked over in our mad rush behind the couch, where we curled up into three tiny balls of shaking target flesh. The shots stopped as quickly as they had

80

started. We checked one another for vital signs, then crawled across the floor toward the kitchen and the back door. My hands and knees bled from pieces of glass and I didn't know whether it was blood that I wiped out of my eyes. I saw the archway to the kitchen and the tile I had sweated and cussed over one energetic summer. A few more feet and we would at least have been in a different room.

Another shot exploded, near my hands, and I collapsed on the floor. Joey Cugie had broken down my front door and popped off a round to stop us. I looked back across my shoulder. Elizabeth's wide-open eyes stared at me, waiting for me to do something. The blur behind her had to be Felix.

He rushed Cuginello and made a flying tackle for his feet. Joey stepped back, raised his hand, and backhanded Felix across the nape of his neck with the butt of the handgun he had used on my house. There was a crack and an echo, like a tree falling in a forest of gangsters, and a gash in the back of Felix's head opened up and let out the blood that had rushed to his brain when he decided he should take on Joey Cugie.

Elizabeth screamed and reached for Felix, but Joey stepped between them. Then he stood on her hands and held her down while he waved his gun at me.

"I'm returning Mrs. Anglin to her husband. You must be the lawyer pal of this other wetback. She's going with me ... voluntarily. Remember that when you give your report to the police. Isn't that right, Mrs. Anglin?"

It looked to me as if he twisted his shoe, but I couldn't say for sure.

Elizabeth wrenched her hands free. She adroitly rolled away and stood. Joey slipped his gun into his shoulder holster and reached for her. She lashed at him and one of her high heels stabbed his shin. He shrieked, doubled over, and massaged his two-hundred-dollar pants.

81

"You lousy bitch." It was all he could say.

I stood and made a move for him, but Elizabeth stopped me.

"No, Louie, let him be. This is between Trini and me; it has been for a long time. Don't get into it any more than you already are."

She reached for Felix and looked at his head. She took off her scarf and wrapped it around his wound. She grabbed my hand and had me hold the scarf in place.

"This is just to slow the bleeding a bit. Call an ambulance and get him to an emergency room."

"What are you doing? You can't go with this creep."

Joey sat on the couch, pale as mayonnaise, but he held his gun again. The last time he had put it away he'd paid a high price.

She walked to the door. Joey stood and waited for her to leave. She looked at Felix and then at me.

"Tell him it was the only way. Tell him it's over. Trini won't do anything else to him; I'll see to that. He knows he won. Take care of Felix."

She carefully opened my busted door and walked out. Joey limped after her. Felix moaned in my arms. I dialed 911.

10

---

*T*hat long, tiring day grew even longer and more tiring. I followed the ambulance to Denver General and did what I could to verify that someone would look at Felix before he bled to death. Eventually, I told my story to a young, athletic blond detective—Sam Harris. The cop had waited for me to finish with the details of checking Felix into the hospital, so I tried to focus on what I thought he should know. I wasn't sure what else Anglin had planned for Elizabeth and Felix and I didn't want to stir up any more blood than necessary, especially any of mine. Harris left to check out my version of the night's events.

I was floating on three hours' sleep and my eyelids felt like pieces of thick sandpaper by the time a bleary-eyed young intern brusquely informed me that Felix had ended up with a minor concussion and a dozen stitches across the back of his head. Felix had to stay for observation at least through the night.

I took several deep breaths. I was a character in a gritty morality play, pushed and pulled by the other actors, and yet I had the unnerving sensation of watching everything happening while I stood around and tried to make sense of it all. I rationalized that my detachment sprang from the lack of sleep, the epinephrine rush from Joey's visit, and my very mixed feelings about Felix and Elizabeth. There were no more hospital details for me to attend to, so I let my body and mind relax, with the expectation that in another twenty minutes I would be home in bed.

The click from the unlocking car door coincided with Harris patting my shoulder. He cornered me in the parking lot and I had to retell the sordid story of the kidnapped wife. When I finished, he flipped through a dog-eared memo book and marked a few pages with the stub of a pencil.

"I guess you can go, Mr. Montez. Some of our men are at your place, so you'll have to talk to them, too. We found Mrs. Anglin and she appeared to be all right. I talked to her myself—at home with her husband. She admitted there had been an argument but said it was cleared up and now she was back home."

He paused for effect, and that irritated the final drop of good manners out of me. I was too tired for the charade. He must have noticed my impatience.

"She and her husband were fairly chummy. No sign of this guy Cuginello. Anglin said he hadn't seen him for several days. Mrs. Anglin said that Cuginello had left in his own car and that she drove home and hadn't seen him since."

"Did she ask about Felix? Say anything about the assault on him or my house?"

"Sure, but she says it was all Cuginello. That he had a thing for her, that he seemed to be drunk, and that she talked him into leaving by promising to meet him at a downtown bar. That's when she left your place, went home, and made up with her old man."

"Did you check that bar?"

Blondie nodded. Why did I flash on the Beach Boys?

"Sure, right away. The joint was closing up. There was a

car in the parking lot that no one claimed and we're running a check on it. May be Cuginello's, don't know yet. But he wasn't around. Our men are watching it, just in case he comes back. So far, nothing."

"What happens now? How about Felix and his headdress of bandages and my house redecorated by thirty-eight slugs? Nobody even gets brought in for any of this?"

"Well, Mr. Montez, you know how these things work. We'll investigate what happened at your house, and, like I said, we're looking for Mr. Cuginello."

Another short pause. My teeth grated against themselves and my fingers squeezed blood out of my keys. Harris stepped back a fraction of an inch.

"But the funny thing is, Mrs. Anglin didn't want to complain. She looked damn inconvenienced when I talked with her. And she told me flat out that she didn't want to see Mr. Grr—what is it, Grr-ara? Anyway, she didn't see him get hit."

"She didn't?"

The exhaustion I had kept at bay for most of the day dropped around my shoulders like a fishing net. I tried to zero in on what Harris said. It wasn't easy.

"She said that Cuginello followed her to your house. She claimed she needed your, uh, legal advice about an Anglin business project and that Grr-ara showed up a little later. Apparently, both of them had been drinking and there was an argument—no doubt about that. Cuginello fired off a few shots, mainly to keep Grr-ara at bay, according to Mrs. Anglin. That's when she took off and, like I told you, that's when Cuginello also left. It's a contradiction with what you've told me, I'll give you that, but until I talk to both Grr-ara and Cuginello, I'm not really sure what happened."

He put his pencil in his shirt pocket and made moves to leave.

"Mrs. Anglin is an attractive woman. I can see why your

85

buddy and Cuginello might have had a dispute over her. Have to be a crazy man, though, to play around with anything that belongs to Trini Anglin. Between you and me, it looked pretty sweet for the two of them, Anglin and the missus, of course. I got the definite impression she was relieved to be back home. And he had a smile that lit up his living room. You know what I mean?"

That's the way it was that year—one crazy thing after another.

The house could have been the scene of the latest Schwarzenegger movie. Bits and pieces of my modest material possessions lay scattered and shattered in the oddest places—funny how a handful of bullets and a gorilla with an attitude can move things around.

I tried to create some order out of the chaos, but an official-sounding knock stopped me. A few of Harris's pals authoritatively stared at me when I gingerly opened the busted door, and they stopped me from changing the crime scene in even the most trivial way. They had returned to finish their initial inspection and chat with the victim. I had to tell my story again and put up with them for a couple of hours while they did their jobs, and that only added to the mess.

Around dawn, they finally pulled out. I tried to talk one of them into giving me a hand with the door, but it was obvious he knew I represented Jenny in her lawsuit against the department, and he wasn't too eager to be helpful. I managed to hang an extra hinge on the door and patch up the window with cardboard and a few boards I kept around for just such emergencies. I felt as safe as I could under the circumstances.

I doubted that Joey would return—there was nothing I had now that he or his boss wanted, and they weren't the types to escalate the small-time menacing charge, especially since kidnapping seemed out of the question.

I had a hard time deciding whether I wanted whiskey or coffee. Sleep didn't appear to be an option. I prepared a pot of coffee, threw in a spoonful or two of cinnamon, and collapsed into a rusty lawn chair on my patio. I watched the last few minutes of the sunrise and was able to catch the changing colors and shadows between the downtown buildings as the city woke up to yet another beautiful spring day in the Rockies. The trees that surrounded the neighborhood were loaded with chirping birds—sparrows?—and I could hear my neighbors starting cars, turning on sprinkler systems, picking up newspapers. From somewhere across the alley, the teasing smell of frying bacon floated across a fenced yard where a pair of dogs barked and whimpered.

Only a few days before, in the midst of a cold snap, I had been busy playing lawyer, on the verge of settling one of my biggest cases—a case with a conscience, talking big deals with fancy firm guys, and life grooved. Then I'd watched that damn pool game and ended up with a black eye. That wasn't enough for Felix; he had to drag me into his love life. The next thing I know, I'm on the floor of my house, dodging bullets. And, of course, the woman at the center decides to act coy with the police and apparently is living happily ever after with the number-one guy in the Denver rackets, while Felix the Sap is under observation with a major-size headache, suspected by the police for at least some of the hassle.

I decided I had to salvage as much as I could. I made notes to call Jenny and arrange another meeting. I couldn't let her pass up her shot at a piece of justice, even if it meant a showdown with her son. I would talk with Felix and try to set him straight one more time—he really *was* better off without Elizabeth. He would not welcome my meddling, but he had come to me in the first place. His affair had cost me at least a good night's sleep, and I was sure I would have to act a little crazy with my insurance

87

company. I also guessed I would have to talk to Anglin himself, with or without Elizabeth, and make sure that he called off the city dogs and allowed Felix his peace. I had to be square with him and clear the air between us so that we had an understanding. I didn't need any more heat from him or his goons.

The promise of the dawn paid off and the morning was beautiful—crisp and clean before traffic and business corrupted it. My head cleared and I actually believed I had a fix on the recent events. I had a simple, straightforward plan. Too bad I never did get the chance to put it into play.

11

The next few days vanished in a surge of activity centered around my practice. I scrambled to make a living. I
realized I enjoyed dealing with the problems of other people, especially when I actually made a difference: divorces,
bankruptcies, a couple of immigration hearings, a bit of
contract work.

Cora Lee Hawkins called, just to let me know that Jessee
was trying to get back in her good graces—and other
places, I assumed—but so far she had resisted his charms
and threats. She didn't want me to do anything. She was
sure she could cope with him. I praised her fortitude.

I left Felix to his recuperation at Denver General and
assumed I would talk to him later. I put off Anglin until
after my talk with Felix. Jenny ignored my phone calls. I
did manage to make a claim with my insurance company
for the damage to my house. The agent wanted to talk to
his lawyers about restitution from Mr. Cuginello. I wished
him luck.

On Friday afternoon, in the middle of assorted paper-
pushing, Evangelina announced that a man wanted to
see me. In my office, that can happen, and does, quite

often. I can't rely on walk-in business, but every little bit helps.

"Did he say what he wants?"

"No. His name's Rick Martínez and he's looking for Felix Guerrero."

My hands tingled as if I had grabbed a pincushion and squeezed. I hadn't forgotten, but I reminded myself anyway that my Walther PPK sat neglected in the bottom drawer of my desk. What I couldn't remember was whether it was loaded.

I gamely shook off the nervousness with the comforting thought that Anglin wouldn't be so careless that he would try to get to me in my own office in broad daylight. Some comfort.

Martínez had shaggy, bushy hair, more gray than anything else, stretched into a ponytail. His eyes wandered along a distant horizon without focusing on anything specific and his hands shook slightly, almost imperceptibly, but constantly. My nervousness returned. He was dressed in a style somewhere between poor college nerd and homeless utilitarian. I thought he must be at least ten years older than I.

He introduced himself in a laid-back voice with just a hint of a Mexican accent. "Appreciate you seeing me like this."

"No problem. What can I do for you?"

Martínez's words rushed out as if his mouth might forget what his brain wanted to say.

"Well, like I told your, uh, secretary, I'm looking for Felix Guerrero, and I been told you're a friend of his, and I thought, well, I thought you might help me find him—it's been a long time; I really need to see him."

His head bobbed up and down and the shake in his hands had increased in tempo to the point that his tarnished wrist ID bracelet tinkled to a tune real close to "Jingle Bells." I caught myself nodding to his beat as I listened to the flow of words. The man was in a definite hurry. He reminded me of Frank from the diner. A dozen questions popped into my head, but I doubted he could answer them, or that he had the time to respond.

I tried one, anyway.

"How do you know Felix Guerrero?"

He didn't stall or search for his reply. He wasn't trying to hide anything.

"The service—marines. We were in Nam together, a long time ago. I heard he was back in town. I . . . I have something to say to him that I think he should hear."

I had him sit down and offered him a soda or cup of coffee. He accepted the coffee and it seemed to help him relax. I listened to his story about his war days with Felix.

"We were in the Third Marines, late sixties. The same recon team. We saw action in the mountains around Khe Sanh, real close to the DMZ. We were dropped in by chopper and we'd stay in the field for four or five days. Me and Felix saw a lot of shit, took more than our share of fire."

"You haven't seen him since then?"

"No, and that's it. Guys always talked about keeping in touch, maintaining contact. But nobody did. After we got back home, it was easier to try to ignore what we had been through, but none of us can . . . not really."

"What brought you to me?"

"That's kind of funny. I was in court, a little trouble I'm fixing up, and I saw you representing somebody on a bullshit charge. I thought you looked smooth, so I asked around the courthouse about you. A guy told me your name and I remembered Felix talking about you, one of his high school partners. It was years ago, but some things stick with a guy, and I recall a lot of what Felix told me, some of the craziest things—stupid details that stand out even now. I . . . can't explain it." He forced his eyes to look in my general direction as he caught himself wandering off. "I asked around at the place I hang out, Joe's Capri,

and sure, they knew Felix and your name rang a bell, too
. . . lawyer pal of Felix and the pool-game fight and you, uh,
you know."

He was making me nervous again, so I tried to steer him
back to the point.

"What is it you want with Felix?"

For the first time since he had walked into my office, he
was quiet. He thought over his answer for a minute, then
launched into it.

"Fuck it! I might as well tell you, no reason not to. Not if
I want to find Felix."

"That's up to you."

"Yeah, right." He put down his coffee cup. He was clear
and precise as he talked about his life in the war. "Out
there, in the field, it was another existence, with different
rules and ways of acting. I'm not making excuses; it's just
the way it was. Most of the time, we had only a half dozen
men in our team. We were all kids, no one older than
twenty, mostly Chicanos and *mayates*. We were always
tired, and thirsty. Sometimes we forgot about food. There'd
be days when we wouldn't even talk to one another. We
just marched in the jungle, our hands on our weapons,
expecting VC around every tree, behind every clump of
rock or mud. Everything we did was to survive. Our job
was to call in artillery on the enemy if we found him. Most
of the time, we didn't, but when it happened, someone
always got killed. And we were sitting ducks for am-
bushes."

Felix had never talked to me about his experiences in
Vietnam. The war for me had meant marches and rallies,
almost getting run over by a semi driven by an hysterical
patriot who decided to disrupt a peace demonstration in
his own special way, and the gassing and beating a group
of us somehow lived through at the Chicano Moratorium
in East L.A. in 1970. Most of the people I knew had had

little, if any, obvious connection with the war. Now Vietnam had walked into my office.

"We had hooked up with another team right before the VC hit us. Trapped for hours. We set up a half-assed perimeter, but we just waited for the Cong to overrun us. Snipers and mortar fire, and men falling all over the place. Felix was only an E-Four, but by the end, he was the highest-ranking guy left."

The man carried the war in a bag of motley, blood-stained memories and images. He brought them out for me one by one.

"Felix decided we needed to move out. Just like that. We thought he was crazy. Where would we go? We knew we were trapped; we were just waiting for something to happen. But he didn't see it that way. He said that we were dead for sure if we didn't try to get out of there. He got real gung ho on us, real marine."

Martínez described Felix's plan, what there was to it. He had needed a diversion, something, or somebody, to keep the enemy busy while the rest of his men tried to run for it. It was a long shot. The men believed that there was no way they could avoid the Vietcong in the jungle, and they told Felix that his plan was doomed. But he insisted, and he picked two soldiers to stay behind. Their job was to convince the enemy that they were the entire group.

"The guys who had to stay behind . . . they knew they were dead. There was no hope, even though Felix promised he would get back with help as soon as he could."

"Did they make it?"

Martínez's eye movements stopped. He looked directly at me.

"They were overrun, never had a prayer. We went back in a few days later. We found what the VC had left and took care of them."

"Felix must know this. Why do you need to see him now, after all these years?"

Evangelina knocked on the door. She entered and politely told us that my next appointment was waiting. I asked her to give me a few minutes with Martínez.

He picked up where he had left off.

"Like I said, it was a different world, different rules. Felix got us through. He kicked our asses through the jungle and we humped all night. We made it. So we should have been grateful."

His pause made it obvious that gratitude wasn't practiced much by him and his fellow grunts. He sat hunched over in my chair as if protecting himself from a jungle downpour, his weapon secured between his legs.

"But we hated him. Those men he picked . . . they were Chicanos. They had been around for a while, almost short. We thought that was wrong. He should've nailed new guys, guys we didn't know, the guys we ignored because we knew they were going to get it. And the *raza! ¡Más coraje que la chingada!* Why pick bros to be butchered? Why not the gabs or *mayates?* One of them was my *carnal, mi camarada.* I made a vow to my homey before we pulled out. I promised him that Felix would die, too."

I listened as he calmly told me he had promised his friend that he would murder my friend. The office seemed very cold.

He picked up on the concern that must have washed over my face.

"Wise out, man. I'm not after Felix. It took me years to get all that out of my system. But I can deal with it now. I'm not totally right, not exactly copacetic, never will be. But I've made my peace with a lot of what happened over there. I'm not a strung out vet ready to freak. I'm not in great shape, but *aquí estoy.*"

"So now you want to . . . what, apologize? Tell him he was right? The truth is, I doubt that Felix needs to hear any of that. It's been over for him for a long time."

"I'm sure you're right. And I guess it's not Felix who

needs to hear any of this; it's me. I need to hear myself tell Felix that it's all okay. He did what he had to. He saved my ass and a few others, and whatever happened back then is done and over. I only want to square it with him, and with me."

I didn't trust Martínez, and I told him so. That didn't faze him and he said he would wait for my call after I had talked to Felix. On one of my legal pads, he scribbled his name and a telephone number, along with "Room 240, LoDo Hotel."

Two hours later, I sat behind my desk, trying to convince myself that I hadn't imagined the events of a few nights earlier and that Martínez's visit was not a late-afternoon dream I had conjured out of boredom. Police sirens wailed across the Northside. The view from my brand-new office bay window included busses rolling down Federal Boulevard, packed with bank tellers, secretaries, and cashiers on their way home to dinner with the family or a night out with the latest personal attachment. I had no plans, again. I had done as much as I could endure on my work, and another night of sitcoms didn't particularly perk up my ears. I found Evangelina at her desk, ready to leave.

I could have asked about something relevant, maybe even personal, and the answers might have started me on another road of complications. But I managed only to say, "Evie, you know anything happening tonight? Music, or a play?"

There was a smirk in her tone. "Looking for something to do with your date?"

I shook my head too quickly and she smiled. She corrected herself. "Or just looking for something to do?"

"You know how it is. Maybe you can suggest something different, give a lead to your boss."

She put on her coat and switched on the answering service by pressing a button on the phone. I thought I

95

detected a blush on the underside of her chin, but it must have been the lighting. She turned to the door.

"I don't know of anything real interesting. Not that you'd like, anyway. Jenny told me she's having a party for Victor at her house; it's his birthday. But that's for his wild friends. I wouldn't go to that for anything. And I can't imagine you there with those hoodlums. Guess you'll just have to rent a movie. Goodnight, Louie. Have a nice weekend."

She was gone, leaving me with the image of her ankles beneath her long black coat and the skirt that at the beginning of the day I thought might have been a little too short for the office.

I weighed my options, decided I didn't have any, and started on my delayed follow-up with Jenny. I wasn't invited, and the CRB surely would escort me right through the house and out the back door, and dump me in the alley if I was lucky, but I thought I might as well take a stab at it and try once more to get through to Jenny. Her case was important enough to take whatever risk the CRB threw at me, and besides, I reasoned, just how crazy could it get at Jenny's?

Around nine that night, I found out.

Young men and their dressed-out ladies stunted with each other in an easygoing, arrogant, almost belligerent fashion, cutting one another with barbs and jokes forgotten as soon as they were said. The CRB members bounced and crowed. I thought I had walked into the party unnoticed. No one hassled me. The girl who opened the door for me smiled at my sport coat and tie and let me in, apparently deciding that my harmless-looking outfit should let me in anywhere.

Young Chicana eyes cruised my face for a clue of recognition, but they didn't linger. I was older than their attention span and not interesting enough to risk the wrath of the strutting peacocks. The boys checked me out and then ignored me when it was obvious I didn't present a threat to their women or turf. I filled a paper cup with beer from a keg sitting in a tub of ice in a corner of the room.

The Rockies paraphernalia was noticeably absent—replaced with party threads—and I figured the boys were off duty and didn't need their work clothes.

A steady beat reverberated throughout the house, shaking the walls and my teeth. I couldn't imagine dancing to it, but the mass of jumping, glistening brown bodies in the front room graphically demonstrated the limits of my imagination.

The days when I would have fit in this party scene were long gone. As I watched the crowd build to overflowing, I could almost see bright dividing lines for the sections of my life—jigsaw-puzzle pieces spread across the floor, kicked and shoved under Jenny's dumpy couch by the dancing feet of young *raza*. My good-time days with Felix at house parties on the Northside had involved smooth but tense excursions into immature bravado. Then I'd graduated to college parties—different jams, different styles, especially in the days of political thunder and lightning when I cruised at another level behind high-octane *mota*. Now, I attended parties because of the need to connect with a potential client, or pump the sweaty hand of a judge, or publicly cut open my veins so the assorted bloodsuckers who hovered at those affairs could swoop down on the ethnic professional and slurp my last drop of *chicanismo*.

I felt a bit lost, almost nostalgic, at this gathering of barrio warriors and their princesses, where no one wanted a piece of my wallet and I wasn't obligated to circulate my business card.

Jenny grabbed my hand and led me into the kitchen, away from the noise. She did it so quickly and effortlessly that I thought she might be ready to hear what I needed to say.

"You stupid son of a bitch! What is it with you, Montez? Victor and Petey will be here any minute. I know what they told you. I can't help you if they decide to fuck you up. You're crazy, man! Crazy!"

A commotion in the other room interrupted my snappy comeback. The heightened level of noise and anxiety transformed Jenny's eyes into sputtering candles at the end of a midnight Mass. A pretty, long-haired Chicana wearing golden crucifix earrings ran into the kitchen, directly to Jenny.

"The Galapago Bloods! Victor and Petey! They're outside! A hassle at the park, now they're here! The guys and—"

The earsplitting pop of a series of gunshots stopped her in midsentence. She screamed and rushed back to the front room. Jenny looked at me for an instant and I saw something like a prayer in her eyes. I ran after her. Shouts and screams filtered through the still-pounding music. Girls and boys, sobbing and cursing, sprawled on the floor, behind chairs and overturned coffee tables. The smoke and smell of the combustion of spent bullets pierced my nostrils and left a sharp tinge of blood and hate.

Jenny stopped suddenly and I ran into her. Petey's body stretched across her front porch, blood gushing out of holes in his silk shirt and pleated slacks. Victor cried as he held Petey's head in his arms. The young girl with the crosses in her earlobes knelt on the porch steps in front of the two boys. She held Petey's hands while Petey's blood stained her skirt. Tears covered her face.

A van swerved down the street, the spark of bullets erupting from its windows into the smoggy Denver night sky. A boy of about fourteen stood to my left, staring at the fading taillights. He whispered, "The chumps are dead, Petey. Dead. *Por vida,* Petey. They're dead."

12

*T*he feud between the Galapago Bloods and the CRB
had finally boiled over into Petey's killing. An ambulance
and an army of police arrived at the same time. Several
minutes ticked away before Petey's body was wheeled into
the ambulance and rushed to Denver General in a futile
gesture of frantic emergency care. The cops made an attempt at a show of force and arrested Victor and a handful
of other CRB members. They didn't seem too interested in
chasing after the shooters.

Jenny freaked. She demanded that the police hunt
down the Bloods. I had to restrain her and assure the cops
that I would keep her under control. I didn't want her
beaten again. The officers didn't hide the fact that they
considered patience a wasted virtue, at least for Jenny and
the kids they handcuffed and tossed in the backseats of
their cruisers. All I got for trying to play lawyer was a
threat to be arrested for interference.

Before he was taken away, I managed to speak with
Victor.

I said, "Don't talk to anybody. I'll see you as soon as I
can. I have to take care of your mother."

The kid had regained his self-control and bottled up his pain over Petey. Jail obviously didn't threaten him. His eyes stared through me and I wasn't sure he cared whether he ever saw me again.

Jenny's house was the second crime scene for me in a matter of a few days and that meant another round of answering uptight uniformed beat cops and tired, note-taking detectives. The partyers who had witnessed the drive-by shooting and hadn't split into the night were isolated in the kitchen while the rest of us fidgeted in the front room, only a few yards from the pools of Petey's drying blood. The house had been cordoned off with yellow-and-black Mylar banners that warned against crossing the line of the Denver Police Department.

Detectives and uniforms measured the porch, the distance from the street, and the door opening. They sketched the scene and snapped dozens of pictures of the house and the street. Sam Harris eventually showed up, late into the affair, but he did manage to order notification to Petey's family. He didn't act surprised to see me and that confirmed that he knew all about my client and her lawsuit and my role as her advocate. And he knew plenty about her son Victor.

"Jenny's lucky it wasn't Victor. His time's coming. That kid is up to his baseball cap in gang shit. Sooner or later, it catches up to them. Either they blow one another away or we put them away." The lecture ended and he added, as an afterthought, "You know anything about this?"

"What's there to know? Another violent night on the Northside, another dead Chicano juvenile, another debt to be paid back by more juveniles. This didn't used to happen around here. I have a recurring nightmare, Harris. All the kids kill each other and we grown-ups have to go back to what we did before there were gangs and crack and automatic weapons. Remember those days?"

His careless shrug told me he didn't know whether I was

trying to be cute, and he surely didn't care. He extricated himself from dealing with me and went on with his investigation. Forty-five minutes later, I had his permission to go home. Jenny shuffled next to me as I made my way to my car. She had calmed down considerably. She said good night and then shook my hand.

She said, "And thanks for helping Victor. I appreciate that. And he will, too; I know it."

It seemed the most natural thing in the world for her gang-leader son to be grateful to the middle-aged mouth-piece he had threatened with grievous injury only a few days before. Without saying it, we both assumed I would check on him in the morning and appear at his advisement, probably on Monday. It wasn't until I pulled into my driveway and locked the car that doubt crept over me, and I knew I would have a bitch of a time falling asleep. Jenny betted on me to follow through, though. It had become a personal situation between us, no longer business, and I wouldn't mess with that, no matter how much sleep I missed.

Judge Margaret Burgett flipped through Victor's file with the eagerness of a hungry rat devouring a baby bird. Page after page of police reports and Social Service investigations documented Victor Rodríguez's scrimy past and predicted his dead-end future. When she finished, she moved her bifocals from the bridge of her nose to her forehead and tried to rub the exhaustion out of her eyes.

"God. Mr. Rodríguez has more history than the Magna Carta. Everything from truancy to drug dealing and now this. The DA wants him off the streets, and I can't say I blame him. What's your story, Mr. Montez?"

I sat in Judge Burgett's chambers at a large conference table next to Victor and Jenny and across from Assistant District Attorney Taylor T. Giles. The meeting might decide Victor's fate. Because Victor was a minor, the judge had discretion that could be turned into persuasive and authoritative suggestion for either side. I had to pull something out of the ole hat, but all I had come up with was a tag that said MADE IN MEXICO.

Over the weekend, I had tried to convince Victor that somehow he had to impress the judge, give her a hook to come up with an arrangement that would keep him out of prison. I didn't think I had succeeded.

Maggie and I had been law school classmates. She was the only black woman who had graduated with my class— man, she was the only black graduate, period. She was years older than I, but she wore the gray hair and accumulating wrinkles with a great deal more dignity than I had ever managed. She had saved and struggled and fought her way into law school and was finally admitted only after she threatened a lawsuit against the school. The suit didn't have a chance of surviving a motion to dismiss, but it would have exposed the school's abysmal black student enrollment and graduation percentages. I admired her for that and occasionally we had helped each other during our law school purgatory. When she landed a job with the district attorney, I was disappointed. She would have made a great defense lawyer. As it turned out, she made a great prosecutor, and kicked my butt a few times. It didn't take long for her to be appointed to the juvenile-court bench, where she had been ensconced for more than a dozen years.

"Your Honor. Mr. Rodríguez was one of the victims in this case. His best friend was killed and he was shot at by the killers. The Court is aware of his record, but the district attorney hasn't shown anything that requires his prosecution. I'm not sure what the DA's Office expects from my client, or this court."

The assistant district attorney responded without hesitation.

"Please, Your Honor. We've all met Mr. Rodríguez before,

102

and I have to give Mr. Montez credit for keeping a straight face when he referred to Rodríguez as a victim. But the Court knows that our office is committed to the city's antigang programs. We're taking a hard line against all gang members. No reduced pleas for violent crimes, and no excuses because of age. Rodríguez is a well-known gang member. This shooting was a gang incident. The minute he's out, the war starts again. We'd have to be naïve idiots to expect otherwise. I guess what the People are attempting to do is to protect the law-abiding public from wild animals like Rodríguez. If we can keep him in jail, at least the only ones who can get hurt by him or his buddies are other inmates and not innocent passersby."

I started to open my mouth to deliver homilies about the presumption of innocence and due process, but the judge cut me off with a flick of her hand.

"Really, Mr. Giles. You still need a charge, an allegation, at least, of a crime. Or should we throw away the keys— and I'm sure Mr. Montez will argue we're tearing up the Bill of Rights, too—for every kid who ever wore colors?"

Giles grimaced a bit, but he was a regular in her court-room and must have been accustomed to her tempera-ment. He knew what he had to say to score points.

"Mr. Rodríguez is the subject of a major investigation into illegal narcotic sales and distribution." Victor stiff-ened in his chair. Jenny grabbed his hand and squeezed. "I expect formal charges soon against him and several others. All I'm asking is that this court help us keep a wrap on him until we end up in district court and Ro-dríguez is charged as an adult."

Victor nudged me and started to blabber in my ear about a setup, about being clean, and about the bullshit in general, but I whispered for him to shut up. He stopped himself, realizing he had lost his cool. At least none of his pals were around.

"That may be, Mr. Giles. But this court needs more than

your expectations. A formal filing, at least a petition in delinquency, or an order to bind him over to the district court. Until this court sees something resembling the orderly turning of the wheels of the judicial system, I have very few options about what I can do with Mr. Rodríguez."

Unfortunately for Victor, Judge Burgett had a conscience as well as a healthy respect for the niceties of constitutional protections. I knew Victor was not off the hook. She would have to do something. Returning Victor to the streets had to mean more drive-bys, and that meant more dead boys.

"I'm continuing this proceeding for one month. Mr. Rodríguez remains under the jurisdiction of this court, if only for the reason that this court has the power to order the Department of Social Services to file a petition in dependency and neglect, and that is exactly what I'm contemplating."

It was Jenny's turn to flinch. The D and N petition could result in the snatching away of Victor on the pretext that she was not a fit mother. Unlikely, especially since Victor was already seventeen years old, but Maggie knew what she was doing.

"I'm going to keep the bond in place, secured by the mother's residence, is that right?" She answered her own question by glancing at the file. "If I have to, I'll place Victor in a foster home, and if he can't function there, then I'll put him in another institution until he turns eighteen. It may not mean much in the long run, but I *will* do it if I have to. Normally, I would start the process now, but I trust Mr. Montez to guarantee his client's cooperation." I carelessly nodded. Sure, whatever. "To that end, I am ordering Victor Rodríguez entrusted to Mr. Montez's care, control, and custody, at least for one month." I licked my lips and squinted at Maggie. Was she serious? She continued with her order. "I expect Mr. Rodríguez to appear in this courtroom one month from today, at which time I will review the report from Social Services as well as any new information the District Attorney's Office decides to provide me, including, I assume, the status of the ongoing investigation." She cleared her throat and stared across the table at Victor.

"Mr. Rodríguez, I hope you understand that you got a break here today and that I expect to see you without any new incidents or contacts in this file of yours. If you don't show, your mother loses her house, your lawyer has to deal with me directly, and I won't hesitate to drop on you as heavy as the criminal justice system allows me to. Is that clear?"

Victor responded with a polite "Yes, ma'am."

Then she turned to me. "Is that clear to you, Mr. Montez?"

We both knew her order had crossed the line. She didn't have the authority to shackle Victor to me, and she certainly couldn't hold me responsible for what he might do in the next thirty days. I could have had her order tossed out by an appeals judge in a matter of a few hours. And then she would yank Victor away from Jenny and into a foster home, which would push him that much closer to a stretch in Cañon City, where he could tangle with all the Bloods who ever inhabited his sleazy dreams of glory and gore.

I said it as politely as Victor. "Yes, Your Honor. I understand."

I sent Victor on his way with his mother and we agreed to meet later to try to put together a plan for our new relationship. The odds must have been better than six to one that I had seen the last of my little buddy Victor.

Sam Harris stopped me in the courthouse hallway on my way to the Fourteenth Street exit. I assumed he was finishing up details about Petey's shooting and doing his share of the "major investigation" Giles had tossed at

Judge Burgett. He looked as though he had just finished a brisk workout in the gym. His pale skin was spotted with red splotches and slightly sweaty. I wanted to tell him that I never did like beach music.

Harris said, "We better talk. Cuginello and Grr-ara."

I had tried to forget about the battle at my house, but if Harris wanted to keep at it, right on, man. My tax dollars at work.

"We pulled Joey out of Cherry Creek last night. His car sailed over the bridge on Speer. At first, we thought Joey bought it in the crash. Would've been too simple that way, though. The coroner's boys tell me that Joey was dead before he hit the water. Couple of bullets through the back of the head will do that. And from the skid marks and the way the car was totaled, Joey must have been doing about eighty, ninety when he was shot. Somebody who was an awful good shot was on his ass and drilled him."

"I'm not surprised, or broken up about it," I said. "Cuginello had a way about him, you know what I mean? It took a while to get to know him, but once anybody did, they hated the guy."

"Don't be a chump. Talk to me about Grr-ara and I can get on with my job. Don't fuck around."

"Harris, I don't know anything about Cuginello's killing, and I don't care about it. Go round up any of the brass-knuckle crowd he hung with and you probably got a good half dozen suspects. And you know where Felix is as well as I do. We both left him at Denver General a few nights ago, or did that slip your mind?"

Harris leaned in close and stared me down. A couple of people in the hall stood a few feet away, watching as though they were waiting for a bell to ring to start the round. This uneven blip in Harris's character showed something I hadn't anticipated. It didn't quite fit the fun-in-the-sun image I had crafted for him.

"Montez, I only have a few words for you. Remember

you're an officer of the court." There seemed to be a rather large number of people who mentioned that fact whenever they thought I needed a reminder of exactly what it was that I did to make a living. "Grr-ara's skipping from the hospital a few hours before Joey's forehead was splattered across his dashboard is just too coincidental for me. But what really turns my crank is that when I visited the house of Mr. and Mrs. Anglin so that I could speak with the wife, in case she might have heard from your pal, what do I find but that she's gone again. You ought to let your friend know that Trini Anglin made certain remarks, threats you could almost say, about what he intended to do with your buddy's gonads. When you talk to Grr-ara, and I don't have any doubt that you will, you tell him to bring in the lady *and* himself so that we can clear up this thing about Joey. I'll leave the resolution of his personal relationships up to him and Trini. You tell him that for me, Montez. Okay?"

He turned his glare on the gawkers and they scurried away in a faked rush to get on with their lives. I let out the breath I had buried in my lungs. The latest exploits of the Crazy Chicano in Love might have gone over the brink. I started to stammer about not knowing what Felix had been up to, but Harris didn't want to listen. He walked away and I settled into the most comfortable position I could manage on the hardwood benches in the court-house hall.

For about a half an hour, I sunk into a hole of deep thoughts and complex plans. I created schemes to extri-cate Felix from Joey, Elizabeth from Felix, Victor from me, and all of us from Harris. Whatever I did, it had to be done quickly, before Victor had time to gather his soldiers and chase down the Bloods and before Felix had to tangle with Harris or Anglin. I didn't want Harris to give me details about the discovery of another body, particularly the body of a love-struck, middle-aged, out-of-control boyhood

107

friend. I was a spectator at a wrestling match between what I needed to do and what I should do. And then, in one of those brilliant mini explosions of simplicity and clarity, I knew what I would do.

I stretched my cramping knees and found a telephone to call Jenny. I filled her in on what had happened and ordered her to keep her son handy for a trip to the country, without telling him what I was up to. She squawked and groaned, but I held my ground and told her I would pick up Victor in a couple of hours, after I had arranged the necessities with Evangelina.

I made it back to my house to finish up the details for leaving town for a few days. The place was still torn up from Cuginello's visit: broken windows, ill-repaired front door, and chunks of wall and floor missing. But what got my attention was the thing in my living room that definitely was out of place. I had walked in not expecting anybody, since it seemed to me that all the points that needed to be made had been—but what do I know about what's needed and what's not?

Anglin sat on my couch, dressed in a suit that would have cost me the retainers from three divorces and a couple of traffic cases. He was tall and the outline of hard muscles strained against the neatly pressed legs of his pants. His brogues were firmly planted on my carpet and his hands mercilessly gripped the couch cushions. He gave the immediate impression that he was ready to pounce if things didn't go his way.

Anglin's Chicano blood had long ago been diluted with the self-hatred that cruised his veins, and whatever Nita Alvarez had taught her son about the more Latin side of his cultural background had been overcome. But she had not raised a dummy; he had to believe that I would react to his unwanted intrusion. He had to have backup sitting in the dark, waiting for his return. My choices were to test my theory and jump off with Anglin and see where that took us or come up with something more civilized.

I was tired of invasions of my privacy, but I guess I had been a lawyer for too long. I thought I could resolve the matter in a judicious, formal way. I hardly looked at him as I picked up the phone and dialed Harris's number.

So much for judicious. Anglin was next to me quicker than I could finish making the connection to the cops. He yanked the phone out of my hand and held it near my jaw.

"Patience, Montez. No need to get your butt in an uproar. I only want information. Talk, that's all. Isn't that what lawyers do?"

"This is ridiculous. First, the cops want me to spill my guts about something I don't have a clue about, and now you think you can barge in my house and intimidate me. Get the fuck out!"

The eerie laughter might have sounded desperate in another man, but not in Anglin.

"Guerrero and Elizabeth. Where are they? Don't be a prick. I'll find them, and there ain't a damn thing you can do about it, Montez, you silly shit. And if I find you with them . . . well, one less greasy lawyer probably won't be missed."

The greasy crack set me off.

I reached for his neck, but he whacked me across the teeth with the phone. My head bounced like a ball hooked to a rubber band. I shook the bells and lights out of my ears, but before I could focus, he punched me in the stomach and I went down. Where was Elizabeth when I needed her?

He stood over me, laughing that fucked-up laugh.

"Montez, I don't want to do this; I don't even like it. And I'm not going to waste my time playing around with you. I don't expect you to tell me anything, although some of my pals might like to try to get it out of you. Nah, not today. This visit is simply a message for Guerrero. You'll talk to him, pass it on. In fact, I don't have to say anything else. I think you know what I would tell that fucking Mexican if he was here. Right?"

He walked over me and out the door. I watched from between the boards in my picture window as he climbed into a white Caddy filled with leering, laughing men.

A few calls, a bag of essential country clothes, a new message on my phone, and soon I was on I-25 South, heading for the San Luis Valley. My company consisted of a sore jaw left over from Anglin's surprise visit, the remnants of a shiner from quieter, happier days, a box of tapes of oldies and Mexican *corridos,* and a scowling teenaged hoodlum listening to his own music on a set of headphones he had worn since I'd dragged him out of his mother's house.

That's the way it was that year.

13

⬥

*T*he stretch of I-25 between Denver and the exit to Walsenburg is fairly uneventful. I preferred this route to the more mountainous drive that entered the Valley through Poncha Pass and Saguache. Going through Colorado Springs requires a bit of meandering, but the bulk of the trip is direct.

Farther south, Pueblo surrounds the highway with a steel mill, neighborhoods named Dogpatch and Salt Creek, and a population that is almost half Chicano. The city has suffered through hard times and crazy nicknames, some with obvious derivations such as Pue Town and others that only long-forgotten Chicanos would recognize—Skaj Land. Pueblo has a colorful history of hosting the annual state fair, incredibly hot summers, and the occasional arrest of a Mafia character buried in quiet anonymity for years before a mistake or a snitch uncovered him.

I always have enjoyed driving from Denver to the San Luis Valley, especially alone. With music blasting from the speakers I installed under the faded tweed upholstery along the Bonneville's rear window, I could trip out on the mountains to the south and west, the flatland to the east, and the fading cities and smog to the north. Until La Veta Pass, the highway allows speed without any real challenges, so I took advantage by pushing the limits of the four hundred cubic inches under the hood of the tank. It responded well, almost appreciative of the chance to air itself out.

I picked up more speed outside of Pueblo as soon as the outline of the steel plant had diminished to about an inch in my rearview mirror. Two hours out of Denver and Victor hadn't said a word. Getting him into the car had required physical force from his mother and me, and we had nearly come to blows. But Jenny pushed and shoved, hollered and cried, begged and demanded, and when he was finally in my front seat, I took off and planned not to stop for anything—gas, snacks, or bladder relief. Whether I wanted it or not, Victor was my responsibility.

The situation looked bleak to me. I wasn't exactly a candidate for Father of the Year. Whatever success there had been in raising my sons had been provided by Gloria, or by Gloria pushing me. Anything other than a holding action with Victor seemed a bit idealistic.

I had debated about bringing my sons along for the trip, but it didn't seem right. Eric and Bernardo lived in the same city as Victor, but they might as well have been on different planets. They probably listened to the same music, but that was as far as the comparison could go. My boys had their mother, school, sports, hanging out at the mall, Nintendo, and their grandfather. Drugs were around—alcohol, grass, acid, speed—but I knew the boys well enough to believe that the experimenting had stopped and they had moved on to other, less dangerous diversions. At least that's what I guessed from the distant and sometimes estranged vantage point I occupied in our relationship.

Victor was a completely different story and there was

nothing my children could do for or with him. And it could get a little hairy. I was looking for Felix, now wanted by the police and certainly of more than a passing interest to Anglin. Victor had been dumped on me and I calculated that the potential risk waiting for me in the Valley was no greater than what he actually faced in Denver. For good or bad, we were stuck with each other. I owed him an explanation, but what I gave him when he finally put down his headphones and came up for air was a tourist guide's speech.

"The Valley has the oldest towns in Colorado. The Spaniards were here in the 1500s. The town of San Luis was founded in 1851. This place has the oldest church in Colorado. Jack Dempsey was born down here. *Penitentes* and *moradas*. On the side of the road, outside of Walsenburg, is a *nicho* of the Virgin Mary. You can see these all over the Valley. These are our roots, Victor. This is the homeland of Hispanos and Chicanos who can trace their families back for hundreds of years, right here in the Valley."

He gave a cursory glance to the country outside the moving car and mumbled, "Jenny told me about the Valley." He pointedly replaced his headphones.

So much for the trip's highlights.

Felix had a slew of relatives in the Valley—cousins in Capulin, an aunt in Antonito, and assorted nieces and nephews spread throughout the huge, sparsely populated counties. But talking to any of them would get me nowhere. I suspected that he had holed up in a cabin owned by a friend of the family. He wouldn't be too conspicuous, and I knew that it would be useless for me to try to find him by asking around. I had to wait until Felix decided he was ready to talk with me. Then he would clue me in to what he intended to do.

Victor and I rolled out a pair of sleeping bags in the back

room of the home of my oldest sister's firstborn, Michael Torres. My nephew had lived in La Jara since he had escaped from his own troubled youth in Albuquerque over a decade before. He had run away from the New Mexican streets and penal system, as well as from my sister and the rest of her kids. Neither Michael nor I had talked with his mother in years. If anyone in the Valley knew about gang violence, it had to be my short, chubby nephew. I hoped I wasn't too obvious to Victor.

Michael understood the situation almost immediately. He helped us unload our bags from the trunk of my car and tried to generate small talk with Victor. The moody kid wouldn't cooperate, and Michael threw an arched eyebrow in my direction.

Michael's wife, Inez, fixed a quick meal of *posole* and beans, then prepared her children for the next day's journey to Pueblo. Inez had arranged a visit with her family. My long-distance request to Michael for lodging had set off quick conversations, rearranged schedules, and a series of plans that culminated in a trip to Grandma's for the kids.

The two-story frame house served the family well. Although the windows allowed drafts and dust to circulate from room to room and different colored patches of carpet inconsistently covered the floors, the structure was spacious and filled with sunlight. A wood-burning stove took up a corner of the front room and almost every other room had a heater of some sort.

Michael and I talked after I had assured myself that Victor was asleep in his bag on the floor.

He asked about Eric and Bernardo and I responded with generalities about their school grades and minor success in sports. He paid his respects to my father and, in return, I asked whether he had heard from his mother recently. He shook his head and I let it go at that.

114

"Michael, I really appreciate this. I didn't mean to put out your family, but . . ."

"*Tío*, don't mention it. Inez is more than happy to visit her mother, and the kids love it. It's like a vacation. I'm glad to help. But this guy, Victor, I don't know, man. He's bad."

"Tell me about it. These gang-bangers are into some hard shit, Michael. I've got to keep tabs on Victor until we go back to court next month. And I'm working on a case for his mother that I think will mean something important to all of them, if only I can get the work done. But I'm really here in the Valley because I'm looking for a friend."

"Felix Guerrero."

"You know. Is he around?"

"Of course. Most of us heard about his hassle with the cops and the crooks. When he picks a fight, he takes on everybody, no?"

"I'm glad to hear he's okay. I need to talk to him."

"The guy's on the run. How are you involved?"

I gave him a quick account of my recent encounters with Anglin and Cuginello and told him about Cuginello's murder. He stared at me, transfixed by a story that could make sense only in the city.

I continued. "Then there's another strange guy, Rick Martínez. Knew Felix in the war. Told me he wants to talk with Felix to make things right. Something that happened in Vietnam. But I don't know. He wasn't exactly the trustworthy type. He could be working for Anglin, for all I know, or trying to make good on his own vendetta with Felix. And the cops want Felix, too. They think he has a connection to Cuginello's death."

Michael moved his legs and slumped back in his wooden chair. He stared at the wooden beams that stretched across the ceiling of his house.

"Your friend sounds like a very interesting character. Still, he has family in *El Valle*. People around here will give him the benefit of the doubt, until he betrays their trust. Then he'll be on his own. Until then, *¿quién sabe?* I doubt even you will know how to find him until he reveals himself."

I nodded in agreement. I expected to wait for word from Felix. But Michael must have thought he needed to explain.

"You know how it is, *tío.* The Valley people have always been close-knit. It took me years to be accepted. I had no connections to anyone. Our family was from Denver, and Albuquerque. It's like outsiders are from a different country, and maybe they are. This is a unique place, but it's beautiful. I wouldn't be anyplace else, no matter how difficult it gets."

For some of the people in the San Luis Valley, it was amazingly difficult. The poverty line was an aspiration for many families. But there wasn't any self-pity or frustrated recriminations. There was plenty of political organizing, plans for improvement, and a sense of ongoing struggle that kept ambition's fire burning within the men and women of *El Valle de San Luis.*

Michael admitted he didn't know Felix's hiding place.

"But you have to believe he'll let you know how to reach him. You guys are friends, right? Grew up together? While you wait, we can do some fishing, take this delinquent hiking up in the mountains, wear out some of his toughness. It can't hurt, Louie. And it just might help."

I kept my doubts to myself and crawled into the sleeping bag near the snoring Victor. The kid tossed and turned for most of the night. He mumbled incoherent words and noises and by the time the sun brightened the room, Victor had squirmed out of his sleeping bag and lay curled on the floor, uncovered.

Michael had us up at five in the morning. Victor and I were too groggy to complain. We piled into Michael's pickup after a quick cup of coffee and a blueberry biscuit warmed in a microwave.

He sped across the country, into the hills, up toward the streams and lakes where he fished on a regular basis, winter included. I had to give the man credit. He was still young—late twenties—but he conveyed a sense of mature well-being in the way he carried himself, the way he worked his *ranchito* and tended the few animals he raised on the small plot of land, the way he played the hand he had been dealt.

I had helped him out as a boy, younger than Victor, when I gave him some legal advice for one of his many scrapes with the law. If I had predicted any future for him back then, it would have been as a poster on the post office bulletin board. His mother, Graciela, my most errant sister, called me for help on a fairly regular basis. The father had disappeared one day when the bawling kids, hungover Graciela, and the loss of his job coagulated into a pressurized mass and pushed him down the road. For a few years, Graciela tried to find a father replacement in me. It didn't work, but I did manage to establish a relationship with Michael.

He finally rejected the mess he had almost made of his life. He left New Mexico when he realized it wasn't his job to get his mother to stop drinking, and although he had tenuous ties to a gang, he wised up to the fact that he didn't have any real friends on the Albuquerque streets. As far as I could tell, the only reminder that he still carried from those days was a scorpion-shaped scar across his left eyebrow.

Michael explained what we were doing as his pickup stirred up dust and rocks in a spiraling tail.

"We'll go on up to the lake, fish, see what we catch. Tonight, we'll stop by Cándido Alarid's house. There's always something going on. We can spend the night if we have to. *¿Qué dices*, Victor?"

117

Michael slapped Victor on the thigh and laughed. Victor had been feigning sleep in the cab, hedged between Michael and me. He jerked away from Michael and tensed the muscles in his neck at Michael's demonstrative display of familiarity.

"Fuck you, man! Don't ever touch me or I'll . . ."

I shouted for Victor to shut up. But Michael didn't need my interference. He jumped on the brakes and the truck fishtailed in the loose gravel as it squealed to a stop. Before the vehicle was completely still, Michael had leapt from the cab and stood on the side of the road, smiling at Victor. He spoke to Victor through the open door.

"Come on, kid. You're a tough guy; come out and take care of me. I won't mind giving you a quick lesson in manners."

I couldn't believe it. I had been ordered by a court of law to keep Victor out of trouble for thirty days at least, and the guy I thought could help had just challenged him to a fight!

I grabbed at Victor, missed him, and got hung up on the passenger door handle. Victor threw himself out of the truck, straight at Michael, and landed with a thud on Michael's shoulders. Victor swung his bony fists at Michael, but Michael quickly gained the upper hand. He wrestled the city boy into the dirt. Victor continued to struggle. I freed myself and ran around the pickup. I watched the performance, rationalizing that whatever had to happen, would.

The fight went on for about ten minutes. Michael wrestled. Victor grunted, cussed, sweated, and infrequently broke free from Michael. Then he would jump back into the fray and get tangled up again in another of Michael's holds. Victor tried to convince Michael with his fists, and a few of these punches landed on Michael's chin, but they produced no tangible result. Finally, Victor, breathing hard, his hair, clothes, and face covered with chalky dust and his elbows and jaw scraped raw, stood before Michael.

Michael said, "Okay, Victor, that's enough. Get back in the truck and then we'll catch some fish."

Victor shook his head. A trickle of blood oozed out of his left nostril, but he ignored it. He said, "You hick mother-fucker. If I had my boys, my machine, I'd frost you right here in the shitty mud and—"

Michael stepped up to Victor, cocked his right arm, made a fist, and, with one solid punch, smashed Victor in the nose, teeth, and jaw. My ward spun in the dirt and tottered in front of me, his eyes straining to focus on my boots. I reached for him, but he fell backward onto the ground—unconscious. I stared at Michael.

My nephew rubbed his knuckles and patted dust out of his clothes. "Help me with him, *tío*. We can lay him out on the bed of the truck. He'll be awake by the time we get to the lake." And he was.

14

◆

Cándido Alarid sat in a rocking chair on his porch. A hand-sewn quilt covered his shoulders and a straw hat that reminded me of my father's fedora shielded his eyes from the sun's dying orange rays. He was surrounded by women relatives of all ages, from infants to *viejitas*. The tanned old man's eternal smile curled into the squint etched in his skin from years of working under the sun. Throughout the evening, I heard his voice above the others. His requests were infrequent, polite, but acceded to immediately. He used terms and phrases that were unheard in Denver—older versions of words, more formal, more Spanish than Mexican or Chicano.

The frame house had been built in a small box canyon, up against picturesque *peñascos*, miles from neighbors, towns, and county sheriffs. Hours before, the Alarid and Martínez clans had butchered a young goat. A duo of cousins who had done the cooking for years prepared the meat with herbs and seasonings. It was wrapped in tinfoil and burlap sacks, buried in a smoldering pit in the yard, and covered with hot coals and embers.

The fishermen had shown up in time for *cabrito* and

beer. We needed it. We were hungry, thirsty, and tired—and successful. Michael insisted on sharing our catch with our hosts. Fried cutthroats and browns were added to the menu.

I am not an outdoors man. I don't hunt, rarely fish, can't hike, and wouldn't know how to survive in the woods. On some nights, I have a hard enough time making it through a parking lot to my car. But the people in the Valley take for granted their natural and rugged activities. They also take for granted that their way of life is sacred. To be honest, I always believed that the rural charm of the San Luis Valley was overplayed: too rustic for my comfort level.

As I sat on a wooden crate near the fire in the Alarid backyard, using my teeth to pick clean goat bones, eating plate after plate of fish, potatoes, beans, and chile, and slugging down beers, I almost came around to accepting the Valley as God's private reserve. But the mosquitoes swarmed over us in droves, eventually driving me to light up a cigarette as an antibug device. A breeze whipped sparks out of the fire as night closed in, cutting through my denim jacket, and I remembered that in winter the thermometer rarely made it above freezing and often stayed at zero or below. And although the Alarids and Martinezes offered an abundance of food and drink, the families had to rely on food stamps during the many months when there was infrequent work.

Through the glow of the fire, I watched my ward try to make himself invisible, although he stuck out like a prune in a basket of strawberries. His reluctance to mingle did not prevent a group of girls and boys from making tentative approaches. Eventually, he begrudgingly introduced himself and seemed to carry on a conversation. He spent most of his time with one of Cándido's granddaughters—Ana, a year away from college in Boulder. Victor was at a distinct disadvantage. His eye resembled mine of the past few weeks and his surly personality didn't mean much away from the Northside.

Up at the lake, he had finally managed to catch a fish, after he allowed Michael the chance to show him how it had to be done. He first tried a fly and a bobber. At my nephew's suggestion, he switched to a red devil so that he would have something to do. Casting and reeling in the spinner at least offered a diversion from watching the plastic bubble that didn't move. He was the most surprised guy in the state when a fish actually swallowed his lure. With Michael's enthusiastic coaching, he landed a nice-looking brown.

I didn't expect miracles from our enforced isolation. I knew Victor was a troubled kid, a hoodlum who would revert to his gang mentality as soon as he was surrounded by his homies, dilapidated projects, junked-up playgrounds, drugs, and turf warfare. But I had to believe that the innate goodness of the Chicano and Hispano people of the San Luis Valley would make a mark on Victor—maybe just a scratch in the sand of his soul, but a mark nevertheless.

The goat roast ended with a parade of cars and pickups driving to scattered outlying houses or returning to Alamosa or Antonito. A handful had elected to sleep out in the open. When there were only a few of us left and we started clearing space on the ground for our bags, Cándido made a show of thanking everyone and inviting us to join the family when they again spread out the food and beer. He shook Victor's hand and then mine. He bent close to my ear and made a few comments in English.

"They tell me that this young man here is a wild one. Send him to stay with us for a few months. We'll have him gutting pigs, planting corn and squash, and growing back his hair. Why do they do that to themselves?"

He started to move on to the others when he stopped and gave Victor one last parting shot.

"En la noche sin luna, todos los borregos son negros."
He laughed.

Victor asked, "What was that? What he say?"

"He said that he wanted you to come back and work for him. And he wondered if you ever got even with your barber."

Victor's hand reflexively stroked his head, then played with the rattail that hung below his baseball cap. He spread out his bag and climbed in.

"Good night, Victor."

"Yeah, sure."

I chugged the warm dregs of my beer and popped the tab on the final can in the cooler. Michael and I sat near the fire for several more minutes, not saying a word, watching the wood burn away, chasing the gnats and mosquitoes from our faces. If I thought of anything significant at all, it was probably some disconnected reflection about Felix and his impassioned rush into a love that had turned into a mad race from gangsters, guns, and threats.

We trudged up the hill in darkness. It was a short climb, steep and cold. The brisk, steady wind never stopped. Night chill crept into my bones and stayed there. We quickly passed the figures of Christ in the various stages of the suffering of the Stations of the Cross. It wasn't the time for prayers at the Stations; that would come with the morning sun. But I could not ignore the dramatic metal sculptures that silently depicted the story that rests at the heart of many Chicanos' spirituality—the pain, suffering, and death of the Son of God, all for the salvation of people such as Trini Anglin and Ed Talmage. They *were* included, weren't they? Surely the saved were not limited to the *viejitas, trabajadores,* and virgins trooping up the dusty, dark hill in down vests and wool sweaters.

The idea for the statues and the visitors' center had been the brainchild of the local priest from the village of

San Luis. After years of begging, crying, and pushing, the priest convinced a Valley artist to create the almost life-sized Stations and orchestrated volunteers from Knights of Columbus chapters from around the state to build the center.

I had been told by friends who had visited the site that the effect was beautiful. During the day, the bronze statues of Christ and the other characters in thé Good Friday story reflected the bright sunshine with multicolored rays of light. The breeze added a peaceful musical background, and tranquillity crept into the souls of those who spent anytime on the hill. The Valley rolled out in all directions in a magnificent panorama of *vega*, streams, towns, and villages—a real-life Taos watercolor. On the western rim of it all, the San Juans and Sangre de Cristos, already rooted in earth halfway to heaven, rose through the grand blue sky and powdery clouds to bump against the many saints watching over *la gente del valle*, or so I'd been told.

Mass at sunrise had not been on my list of things to do in the Valley. But Victor had learned from Ana that a special Mass had been scheduled to offer thanks for the completion of the Stations project. Ana, who had slept in the back of a station wagon with her sisters, woke Victor up as her family left for San Luis and invited him. He stuttered his interest to me and I agreed to let him go, as long as I tagged along. It was the first positive sign from him and I grabbed at it. Michael bowed out and stayed sleeping in his bag.

Victor, of course, was under the influence of the scent of Ana. In the city, he would have won over the lady with a whirl of parties and good times, righteous dope, rowdy *vato* grandstanding, and more bullshit than the National Western Stock Show. He had learned that romance was different in the Valley. In the oldest town in Colorado, Victor had to climb hills, camp out on the rocky ground, and wait for the sun so that a priest could preach to him about all that was wrong with his life. If he behaved himself, he might just have a shot at spending a few minutes with Ana, next to her three sisters, mother, grandmother and a couple of aunts. Victor's rep, ever helpful on the streets, had followed him on the interstate and stirred up the guardian-angel complex among Ana's relatives, to the considerable detriment of his *movidas*.

We waited on the hilltop near the visitors' center, trying to keep warm until sun broke across the Valley and the priest started his prayers. Victor and I sat on a rock near the back of the crowd, with a good view of the few lights from San Luis.

Victor was tired and dirty. Michael and I had made him walk miles around the lake while we fished, led him across rocky arroyos, up and down steep ridges, and generally made our excursion more rugged than it had to be. My leg muscles had tightened during the night, stretched out on Cándido's rocky ground, and I assumed that Victor had to feel at least as miserable as I. The altitude, exhaustion, and surroundings might have helped him find his voice. He talked to me about a few inconsequential topics. I kept at him in order to get him to open up. I asked about his mother and the trouble she had had with the police.

"Jenny's been fighting the pigs ever since I can remember. I seen newspaper stories about her. She marched on the jail once because they beat up some guy in the elevator and he lost an eye. Then they arrested her. She's been arrested more times than, uh, than Petey was."

He turned his head into the darkness. I probed as unobtrusively as I could.

"How long you know Petey? From when you were kids?"

He answered quickly, as though talking would keep away the thoughts he had a difficult time accommodating.

"Yeah, man. We grew up together. Petey was my main man, the one guy I knew I could stand with. Some day, somebody . . ."

He didn't need to finish. His tone reminded me of the whacked-out soldier Rick Martínez, who had made the same vow for his dead friend.

"Victor, you've got to move on, man. You're going to end up just like Petey if you don't straighten up. You know that. You see it around you every day."

Victor slid off the rock and paced nervously in the sandy soil surrounding the dying Christ impaled on a cross. The sun peeked over the horizon and unleashed its light and warmth over us. I felt a tiny jolt of comfort, a feeling of distant hope in the first minutes of the day. Victor turned and faced the sun. He spoke without looking at me.

"Montez, it's good what you're trying to do with Jenny. She deserves it. She's put up with shit ever since I can remember. Maybe you can really help her." He stopped while the sun climbed a fraction of an inch. Shadows rolled across the ground, into the Valley. We were all in the sunlight. He said, "Petey died because he was with me. The Bloods want to keep the business that we put out a bid for. They can keep it. Crack selling and crack houses is all it means. The Bloods thought they could wrap it up if they wasted me. They missed and Petey bought it. They had no respect for me or Petey. It's always like that. Respect, man. It sucks."

He lit a cigarette. The priest began the mass and most of the people knelt in the dirt. Victor and I watched from the back, whispering to ourselves.

"It's been going on ever since I was a kid, Victor. You can't make it right; you can only do the right thing for yourself."

"Yeah, sure. Petey told me that once, when we were in juvie together. He said we could only do right by ourselves. We didn't have anyone else except ourselves." That wasn't what I meant, but I didn't try to explain it. Victor would strain his own meaning from anything we said or did in the short time we were going to be together. "That's where we really became partners—in jail. We were down! He saved my ass and together we survived. I'd probably be dead if it wasn't for Petey."

"Yeah. I guess you can die in jail. But you can die in the streets, too, or even up here in the hills."

"You're right, man. It can end anywhere, anytime. And the guys who really run the shit, the guys who make the real money—nothing happens to them. I know those guys. Big fucking assholes. They use the CRB and the Bloods and every other gang to run their stuff, take the heat, and then offer more of the pie to the gang that can take it. That's what it was all about. Petey died because the Anglins put up their business for management by one of the posses. And there ain't a fucking thing I can do about it."

He said it all quietly. And although the sun had warmed the air and the earth, I buttoned the top snap on my jacket to ward off the ice in his words.

"Victor, not everyone has to go down that road."

"What do you know about what I can do or not do, Montez? You're a lawyer. You got it made, man. Petey and I had nothing but each other, and now I ain't even got that."

"Look, bud, I grew up on the same streets. I had my homies, my clique, my run-ins with the cops. But it didn't stop me. I even did time in jail. You don't have anything on me, Victor, except excuses."

He didn't respond. He watched the priest lead the faithful in prayers. He wandered away and ended up near Ana. I wandered away, too, in my head, back to a county jail and an incident from my youth that I hadn't thought about in years. I had dishonestly implied that the sins of my youth were similar to Victor's. The comparison was superficial. I'd never had it as mean as Victor. I hadn't faced violent death when I was a teenager or struggled to find my lost identity through gang colors, hand signs, and turf wars.

Even so, he had unearthed a few of my darker memories, items I had tossed in the back of the closet and now rediscovered because of his swaggering bravado and dangerous insecurity. Thanks, kid.

15

I was twenty years old when I was sentenced to a county jail over Christmas, my penance for the misdemeanor of malicious mischief. Malicious mischief could mean anything. The truth is, I was guilty of burglary, theft, destruction of private property, trespassing, and who knows what else.

The only tangible ramification I suffered for this youthful indiscretion, in terms of its long-lasting effects, occurred a half dozen years later in the form of Judge Barrera when I voluntarily participated in the mental anguish and emotional distress known as the state bar examination. I had to submit to a face-to-face interview with an ethics committee of the bar because of my conviction and, of course, they let the only Spanish-surnamed member of the committee inquire about my worthiness to join their ranks. His Honor glared at me over a copy of my sentencing report as he squeaked out questions.

"Mr. Montez, did this . . . this incarceration have anything to do with, uh, with student demonstrations or, uh, violence connected to the university?"

I assured the doddering old coot that no, my bust was

not a matter of conscience, only an alcohol-inspired outlet for the materialism I had managed to pick up on campus. Barrera seemed pleased with that and the committee passed me.

My crime partner was a rich, if not speedy, white boy from California and, all things considered, we got off easy. David's father flew in the day after our arrest and within a week a deal had been cut. We were college kids and not real criminals, they told us, and so they slapped our wrists. The judge ordered us to spend Christmas vacation as guests of the county.

I could recount the misery of the joint—the abuse I endured at the hands of the screws; the sadistic jailbirds; the convict wars and race riots. But none of that happened in the county jail, at least not that Christmas. I learned how to play pinochle and drink coffee without sugar. No, the time actually wasn't that hard, and if it hadn't been for Juan, I doubt that the experience would have made any lasting impression on me.

My sentence began on a Sunday. The twenty or so prisoners were bunched in a large room in the middle of the cell block, watching a football game on the small black-and-white television bolted to the wall. The cells opened into this main room. Windows with thick iron screens ran along the top of the room, near the crease of the ceiling. Through them, we caught a glimpse of the sky or a few stars.

That first day, I sat in a corner of the central room and tried to read. No one looked at me; no one offered any greeting. The men whistled and cheered, intensely wrapped up in the game. They had no reason to be interested in me. I didn't know how to act or what to say. I had disconnected thoughts about where I was and what I was supposed to do but no clear answers. When I realized that I was not reading the book, only holding it in front of my

130

face, I decided to check out the game. I nonchalantly joined the group.

It was a play-off between Dallas and another team I have long forgotten. When the Cowboys executed a good play, the prisoners went crazy. If Dallas scored, pandemonium erupted. The loudest was the meaty, burly-headed *tejano* who shook his fist at the set and cussed in Spanish when the game went badly for Dallas and who jumped and screamed with childlike joy when the Cowboys finally won the game. I didn't have to be Einstein to know that Dallas was the local favorite because of this guy. The men followed his lead, took their cues from him, and by the end of the game, I was cheering as crazily as everybody else. He was sinister- and powerful-looking, with a darkness that added to the sense of strength I picked up from him. His enthusiasm convinced me that Dallas was a damn good team.

I quickly learned the routine, such as it was. The men hung around the concrete pen reading, drinking coffee, playing cards, or watching television. A few small groups hunched over the tables, talking about things that are important to men trying to impress one another. There were three meals each day during the week, two on Sunday when visitors were allowed. Many of the visitors brought food, which was usually shared by the men during the long Sunday evenings after the football games.

I hung out with Hank, a bony drifter with a crew cut, and dangerous-looking Phil, doing ninety days for drunk driving. Others joined in from time to time, but the three of us made up the core of our circle, based on our relative youth and the nature of our offenses against society. We were not in for long stretches or for heavy crimes. I learned from them that my job in jail was to stay out of the way and avoid whatever was happening in the rest of the cells.

Phil gave me the details about Juan.

"His last name's Salazar. They call him Chato."

I nodded. The moniker was a natural given the man's wide-angle features, which included a broad *indio* nose.

Phil went on with his story. "He blew away Dionisio and Timmy Luna last spring in Madruga's Bar. You musta heard of that. Don't mess with him. They got him here while his lawyer argues some appeal motions from his trial, but it's only temporary. He's on his way to Cañon City, so he ain't got nothing more to lose. If there hadn't been a fight, he probably would have gotten the gas chamber."

The fact that Chicanos killed one another was no surprise, but the times were a-changin', at least that was the rap back in the dorm, and I wondered where Chicano brotherhood, *carnalismo,* fit into Juan's story.

"The Lunas and Salazars have been fighting since Pete Luna shot Toby Salazar ten years ago when he caught Toby screwing his daughter in the backseat of a car. That was a mess, man, let me tell you. The girl—Roberta, I think her name was—went off her nut and ended up in Pueblo at the state hospital. Pete died about a year later, heart attack. Those people have had more fights, knifings, shootings, you name it. If the families run into each other, someone gets busted up, never fails."

"And that's why Salazar shot the brothers? Part of the feud?"

"Well, yeah, it's all part of the same thing, man. But with Juan, it was a little different. Dionisio and Timmy were the younger brothers of Gilberto, and now Gilberto's in the pen doing time for a gas station stickup in Brighton. Everyone said that Gilberto was fingered for the job by one of the Salazars; you know, someone tipped off the cops about where he was holed up and he got pinched with loot from the robbery. The brothers thought that someone was Juan."

He nodded in the direction of Salazar, who casually

stretched against a wall of iron bars, talking with a few of the older men.

"He killed the brothers because they called him a snitch. They had more guts than I have, I'll tell you that. They bled to death in the bar and Juan was arrested later that night, sleeping it off like nothing happened, you know? He's a cold-blooded guy."

"Any Lunas left?"

"Oh, yeah, you know Chicanos, man. Cousins, uncles, not to mention the *compadres*. But things've cooled off since the shootings. Everyone knows Gilberto's waiting in Cañon for Juan; all the scores should be settled soon, one way or another."

Hank was amazed by the stories of Chicano violence. He was from the Northeast and hadn't known any Mexicans until he decided to hitchhike as far west as he could. Winter had stopped him in Colorado. Hank's problem was that he loved whiskey and the way it affected him. When he had that feeling, he enjoyed the company of women who were painted up and sloppy from drink. Too often, the women had men in their lives who resented Hank's friendly personality.

The last one to personally express his resentment was a turkey rancher who drove a red pickup and wore a John Deere cap. His wife had run into town on a Saturday night and it was Hank's bad luck to meet up with her.

I listened with bemused incredulity to his version of the incident that had landed him in jail.

"She just wanted a little excitement in her life," Hank said. "We was dancing, drinking, over at the Front Range Inn, having a good old time, when in walks this rustic, right off the farm. He started hollering at May, calling her a whore, slut, all kinds of nasties. Shit, I didn't even know who he was. You'd think I woulda learned by now; I been down that alley a few times. So I said for him to jump back into his two-bit truck, go home and feed the chickens.

Christ, you know that was the wrong thing to say to a turkey farmer, especially when I got his wife draped all over me, so he grabbed me by my shoulders, lifted me straight up—strong fucker—and tossed me about ten feet. I landed on a table, beer spilled all over me, guys were hollering and cussing, and the next thing, I jumps on his back, holding him by the neck. Heck, that guy about had a fit. He was slapping at me, twisting and turning, trying to knock me off. And May, she was a prize, let me tell you. She starts smashing me with her purse! Damn thing must have weighed twenty pounds. Each time I got spun around in her direction—smack! Right in the head. I passed out after about ten minutes of her knocking me with her purse and him spinning me around. I'm doing six months for disturbance, but I'll be out soon. Good behavior."

Hank walked away, looking to bum a smoke.

I met Juan because of my grandmother's food. After one of their Sunday visits, my father and *mi abuelita* said their good-byes, unable to understand what I was up to, and I turned to the box of food for my chow. I opened cartons of green chile and beans, tortillas and rice, and I was savoring the aroma when he walked up to me. His constant aura of strength and foreboding engulfed me and for the first time in several days I believed I was locked up. The quiet voice surprised me.

"*Oye*, I could sure use some soul food in a bad way, guy. I ain't had nothing decent to eat since they threw me in here."

"No problem, man."

I acted cool, dished food into a paper plate until he stopped me, and then said, "There's more if you're still hungry."

He talked to me during the week after, and each Sunday I shared my food with him. He grumbled about football and bragged about Texas and said I was a lucky guy because my family visited me and hadn't deserted me.

134

"You read too much, Louie. I never knew a Chicano who reads like you. One of these days, I might get into it, you know, read some of those James Bond books, whatever else is good. I like those James Bond movies. You ever seen any?"

"Sure, a couple. That guy has *huevos* of steel, not afraid of anything. A real macho guy."

"Yeah, he's bad, for a guy in *los monos*. Nobody's like that. We got to decide things in our own way. We ain't got secret weapons. Sometimes you just got to throw down."

"Right, man, whatever you say."

He stared at the concrete walls, as he often did, and I left him to his thoughts. He was a killer—no doubt about that in anybody's mind. When he walked around the cell block, he reminded me of a sumo wrestler. He took short, deliberate steps and held his thick arms close to his sides as he paced the room like a caged zoo animal. We watched him from the corners of our eyes, suppressing the fear that one of us would do something to trigger his violence, for then, we believed, we would all pay.

He told me he was originally from San Antonio, although he had grown up in the migrant stream from the Rio Grande Valley on up to Michigan. His first stretch was in reform school at fourteen for stealing a pocketful of money from a drunk. He earned his education in Texas prisons and jails and when he decided his home state was too hot, he drifted north to live with scattered segments of his family. He was made part of the feud because he was part of the family, and that was all right with him.

"I ain't like you college Chicanos." Chato cleared up this point over a midmorning cup of coffee, just in case there was any confusion. *"Iba a la barra, me ponía pedo, y a tirar chingazos*. Typical Friday night. I only got a few things. *Mi familia, respeto*. This *pinche bote* don't mean nothing to me. Everything I did, I'd do again. *No le hace*. That's the way it has to be."

135

He had other interests in addition to defending the honorable Salazar name, football being right near the top of his list. But Juan's great obsession was *la música norteña*, the polkas, *rancheras*, and *corridos* of south Texas and northern Mexico played by the *conjuntos*—bands made up of accordions, *bajo sextos*, *contrabajos*, and guitars—with names like Los Relámpagos del Norte, Conjunto Bernal, Los Desveladores, and dozens more that he recalled in an instant. Without any urging, he would launch into stylized renditions of the greatest hits of these musicians known only to the Chicanos of the Southwest, and then only to the lucky few who chose not to stray too far from their cultural roots.

There was something unreal about the mix of Juan and his music. Just standing near him made me nervous. His bulk and attitude intimidated the bravest of men, and I certainly did not feel the least bit courageous. I jumped when I first heard him launch into a song. But as I listened, I was awestruck by the incongruity of the hardboiled farmworker with the Texas drawl serenading the bedraggled inhabitants of the rural county jail with songs of wronged lovers and misplaced loyalties.

Away from the music, Juan reverted to the incorrigible criminal pose he had carefully incubated through years of lockups and lockdowns, real time and downtime. Once I described my arrest and the clever tricks the police had used to try to convince us to name an accomplice they were sure had escaped. David and I had been the only ones involved.

"The detective said that if we told him who the other guy was, it would go easy on us. He said the county jail was a rat hole, a real dump. We could stay in the city jail and not have to get mixed in with the hard core. We almost bought that."

He laughed at the idea of the police grilling me.

"Yeah, shit, that must have been skinny-ass Lardner.

He thinks he's so smooth, man. It's a good thing you didn't fall for that crap. I ain't never been in a worse place than that city jail. *Estaba cabrón alli el pedo.* You guys could have been over here all that time, eating warm food, watching the games. Clean beds. They had you all by your-selves, sitting ducks. Fucking *placa*'s too much, man, too much."

He paused and I could see him drifting off again. His eyes flared, wide open, and he grabbed me by the elbow and squeezed. I couldn't wrench free.

"It's good you didn't snitch, bro. No matter what they say, what they promise, it's not worth it. Don't even let them talk to you about it; don't let nobody get the idea."

He released my arm and the blood rushed to where his fingers had been.

He made his point again. "I ain't no snitch, man. *No lo olvides.*"

"Sure, sure," I mumbled, but I wanted to ask about the brothers, about the whispers in the cells that said Juan had sent his rival to prison and then killed two young men because they had called him on it and I wanted to ask whether it was worth it, *vato*. But I didn't, and for the same reason I didn't ask about the final confrontation that we all knew had to happen. I could talk to him about music and jails around the country, but Phil had warned me not to mention the Lunas.

"He'll flip out. He's crazy about that shooting."

I saw his anger once. Martin was one of the flakier guys in the jail. I didn't know what he had been busted for, but it must have been a major offense like urinating in the park. He was a loser all the way around. He'd wake up in the morning farting, grunting, and groaning, so that we all heard him. He'd splash water in his face. He never show-ered, just put on a shirt and then spray deodorant in the general direction of his armpits, over his shirt. That al-ways cracked me up. I avoided him because he was strange. Juan, on the other hand, put up with him and let him hang around. They talked as if they had met in another jail.

We were eating lunch when a loud crash from Juan's table stopped us all, frozen at our seats, unsure about what would happen next and not anxious to learn. A metal food tray rattled on the concrete floor. One of the guards looked in, saw the mess, and ignored us. It wasn't his job to clean up after us.

Martin stood, pale-faced and sweating. He was terrified. He started to say something that sounded like an apology, but Juan stopped him.

"Shut up, runt. I told you, I ain't no snitch—I don't care who says it. I never snitched on nobody in my life. I'm gonna fuck you up, man!"

Martin stammered some words, but they wouldn't come out of his constricted throat. Juan reached for him as the smaller man ducked under Juan's arms and ran into his cell. He slammed the door and locked himself in. Juan leapt at the bars of Martin's cell, swearing and hollering in Spanish, but he couldn't get to him. He turned his rage on the trash cans in the room, kicking them and spilling their contents on the floor. Cigarette ashes, newspapers, and old magazines mixed in with the food from Juan's tray.

Nobody said a word. We ate in silence as Juan ran around the room, slapping the bars each time he passed Martin's cell. He hurled epithets at the quivering Martin, who laid on his bunk, crying, saying over and over, "I didn't mean nothin'. I didn't mean nothin'." We relaxed only when Juan stopped, sat down in one of the wooden chairs, and turned on the television.

Martin pleaded with the guards for protection. They had their fun for a few hours, but eventually they relented and moved him to an isolation cell. We didn't see him again.

I can't say I was Juan's friend. I don't know whether he had any friends. He had family—that much was clear—

but no one visited him on Sunday afternoons. The image of two brothers bleeding to death on a filthy beer-joint floor wouldn't leave me and I was relieved when the sheriff told him he finally would be transferred to Cañon City.

The night before he was to be moved, I couldn't sleep. I sat on my bunk, my pillow propped against the wall. I stared into the blue light from the windows in the ceiling of the room. I could see some of the men turning awkwardly on their narrow bunks. The moon was brightest in Juan's cell. I had a perfect view of him.

He stood bare-chested in the middle of his cell. His head was bowed, his hands folded, and I thought he was praying. He stepped out of his pants and I saw the bulk of his flesh in the light. His skin was metallic, his hair plastic-looking, hard and dark. He grabbed a piece of cord from under his mattress, filched from a storeroom watched by a careless guard, and tied it around his neck. He looped it over a pipe that was supposed to be flush with the ceiling but that had been pried loose for the cord to fit. He secured it to the pipe with a thick, complicated knot. He climbed on the top bunk and eased himself over the side.

I realized I should have done something. I could have hollered for the guards, made enough noise to wake up the cell block and save Juan. I didn't act. I convinced myself I was respecting his choice, that it was something he had to do.

He spun in the air and I thought the pipe would break from his weight. His body rotated and first his face and then his back twisted before me. His eyes were open and his hands gripped the roll of flesh bulging around his neck. When he turned, I saw the huge blue tattoo that covered his entire back. It was the Mexican Madonna, Our Lady of Guadalupe, the Blessed Virgin Mary.

I jumped from my cot at the sounds of running men shouting and banging cell bars and metal doors with wooden clubs. Lights erupted and the cell block was flooded with a yellow burst of illumination. Deputy sheriffs rushed to Juan's cell and dragged him away, coughing and crying.

I prayed to the Virgin that night for Juan. I prayed to her for me.

16

Victor and I made it back to Michael's house near noon. Ana Alarid had offered us a ride in her slightly battered station wagon, and Victor accepted for both of us. He hadn't expected Ana's mother, and the old lady stared at Victor the entire trip, never letting him out of her sight. She turned her tiny body in the seat and draped herself across the back of the headrest, her eyes fixed on the young devil from the city. She didn't say a word, but I convinced myself that the old lady knew about curses and spells and hexes, *la embrujada,* and I did nothing to upset or worry her. I had enough trouble on my hands without stirring up the wrath of the Chicano occult.

Ana sat on a pillow in the driver's seat, hunched over the oversized steering wheel while she tried to control the sticking gearshift. The car kept her occupied, but her flitting eyes in the rearview mirror gave away her interest in Victor.

She drove west on 142 in the general direction of La Jara. When we entered the nondescript town limits of Manassa, I said to Victor, "This is the place where Jack Dempsey was born. That's the house where he lived." I pointed and Victor indulged me by looking quickly in the indicated direction, but his heart wasn't in it.

"What is this thing you have about this Dempsey dude?"

I couldn't hold it against him. We had been awake since before dawn. Our backs ached from sleeping on the ground and our legs tingled from the extended hiking of the day before. We were city limp and country ragged.

Our thanks and good-byes to Ana took all of maybe three seconds and then she was gone. Victor stretched out on Michael's couch and the familiar snoring started five minutes later.

Michael had gone off to work at a mushroom greenhouse, where he served as all-around handyman. Mushrooms represented a fairly new idea for revitalizing the Valley's economy and Michael had been one of the lucky few to find steady work in the enterprise. Of course, he also worked for the phone company as a part-time lineman and he filled in at a gas station in Alamosa a few hours every week. A man does what a man can.

My body sank into an overstuffed chair not quite as beaten down as I felt. I knew I should get some rest. For several minutes, I tried to fit into the uncomfortable chair. I stretched my legs when they started to go numb and turned my neck until I was sure it wouldn't crimp up on me. Eventually, my butt fit in a groove in the chair and my eyelids stopped fighting unconsciousness. At what seemed to be the precise instant when sleep overcame me, car tires kicked up gravel in the front yard and someone pounded on a very obnoxious horn.

Felix had decided to look me up. I groggily answered the bleating by throwing open the front door. There he stood next to a tricked-up, snorting hunk of Detroit that clashed with the environment as badly as my outdated suits set me apart from my colleagues in the bar association. The 1964 Chevy Impala Super Sport ragtop was dressed in candy wild cherry with flakes, gold-on-gold wires, and a mural of the miracle at Tepeyac painted across the trunk in iridescent green, blue, and white.

Felix reached inside the driver's window and the horn went off again. A wolf whistle loudly repeated itself and I felt a twinge of pity for any woman who had been its target.

Felix laughed. "What you think, aay? Now here is a ride." His sweeping arm encompassed the car, the Valley, the Southwest. "Heard you were around, soaking up the culture. Nice to see you, man."

I walked into the sunshine and casually shook his hand.

"Where'd you get the wheels, Gato? Kind of out of place, no?"

"My *primo*'s. He's in a car club. A good excuse to get together with the boys every other weekend. Very nice, I think, but you can see it needs a little work."

The paint was chipped in a few strategic locations. The Virgin, for example, had brownish blobs of faded paint for hands and the roses were a dull rust color rather than their original brilliant red. The button-tuck upholstery on the two swivel seats in the front had split at the seams and the velour ragtop boot was badly ripped. But it was a Chicano icon, a chrome-and-metal monument to sensuality, spirituality, and cool, and the flaws only added character. I had to agree with Felix; it was a sharp-looking car.

Felix's smile stretched all the way to the Great Sand Dunes National Monument. I attributed that to Elizabeth. The man was happy. He bounced around the yard, talked with an exaggerated use of his hands, and used up more energy than I thought he could muster. But, like the signs of age in the Chevy, his eyes were tired and wary, and it was obvious that the hounds on his trail kept him up at night. Or maybe that was Elizabeth, too.

"Hop in, Louie. Come on up to the cabin. I need some legal advice. You can write this off as a business trip."

I called Michael at work and explained that I would be gone for the night. He assured me that he would keep an eye on Victor. The two had somehow formed an unarticulated agreement to respect each other. There could be more trouble between them, but that was a risk even if I stayed.

My note for Victor simply said that Michael would return soon to fix dinner and that I would be back the next day. The pencil stuttered over the words, but I reminded him that he remained under my care and control.

Felix roared across the highway, opening up the custom job for all it had in its 327 engine. He had the top down and the screeching wind made it impossible for us to hear anything other than a shout. I tried for a few minutes. I screamed at him about Victor and street wars and my newly acquired status as role model. I said I had to get back and finish my big case against the Denver Police Department. He nodded and cupped his ear with his right hand when he wasn't working the chromed skull that topped off the gearshift. In surrender, I sagged into the bucket seat and made myself as comfortable as I could.

We passed a plate-glass window in a deserted bait shop and I saw the fleeting reflection of a bright paint job on a young man's automobile that carried a pair of out-of-place middle-aged men surrounded by an engine's throb and a dusty cloud of misgivings. Felix had a strange way of making himself inconspicuous.

Elizabeth welcomed me like an old friend. She wore jeans and a sweatshirt, no makeup, and her skin had a dry, tight look from what the local chamber of commerce called the Valley's "cool sunshine." Dark smudges under her eyes confirmed that she and Felix had missed out on several hours of sleep. I hoped I never had a nightmare about Trini Anglin.

"Have a beer, Louie. I'll fix something to eat."

144

"Thanks, Elizabeth. That ride did make me thirsty."

Felix made sure the stove had a good fire. He added a handful of *palitos* from a box full of chopped wood. Elizabeth started dicing onions and garlic.

In a few minutes, Felix and I sat around a table, drinking beer, eating potato chips, and trying to act as if everything was normal, just another day in the life of Felix the Cat, Elizabeth the stolen wife, and lucky Luis Montez.

He answered my first question before I asked it.

"I had to leave town, man. Somebody tried to kill me in the hospital. I woke up under a pillow—no air, no light, nothing. I guess I was lucky that whoever it was wanted to do it quietly. He could have shot me easily. There weren't any cops around. I managed to break away and hit the motherfucker a good one, but he ran off. A nurse—a student actually, not a real nurse—finally heard the noise and tried to stop me from leaving. She claimed she didn't see anybody. I don't know how she didn't hear us crashing around the room or how she avoided smashing into the guy tearing ass down the hall, but, hell, maybe she was taking care of another patient. Maybe one of the doctors." He chuckled. "Anyway, I took off as soon as I could, before the police showed up again, or the guy who tried to smother me."

"Harris thinks you had something to do with Cuginello. What about that?"

Elizabeth answered from the stove as she dumped the remains of a bag of spaghetti into a pot of boiling water. "Joey died the same night Felix was attacked. Felix called me after he sneaked out of the hospital. He thought I was in danger. Trini's crazy. He could do anything. We were lucky that he wasn't around when Felix called. I left, we got together, and we drove out of town without thinking, without planning anything. We didn't even know about Joey until we read it in the papers. Joey could have been killed by anyone, even Trini. Maybe Trini got mixed up and believed the story I told the detective. If he had any, he might have decided to defend his honor. There always was trouble between him and Joey."

The fairy tale she'd told Harris about the dueling lovers—Joey and Felix—had eaten at my guts when I first heard it and I didn't feel any better after her glib account of the reason for the disappearing act. Elizabeth, however, treated it as the most natural way for her to work herself out of a jam with her old man. Felix kept his opinion to himself.

A rifle and a handgun rested on Felix's jacket, near the door. He answered my look by saying, "We spent the morning at target practice. Elizabeth's an excellent shot, almost as good as I am. Just in case, man."

I shook my head in obvious disapproval.

"What do you intend to do? Sooner or later, you have to straighten up the mess in Denver. You can't hide away from Trini forever. And, if you really want legal advice, I have to tell you to turn yourselves in to Harris and let him figure out who did Cuginello. This is crazy—even for you, Felix."

"No lectures, man. We're leaving. We're going to start someplace else, and that's it."

There had been times when I admired his stubbornness. "Anglin won't let it happen. He already tried to kill you at the hospital. Somebody nailed Cuginello, and I don't think it's just a coincidence that it happened on the same night that someone tried to take you out. And a guy named Martinez from your old marine outfit is looking for you, too. He was spooky. He could've been the one that tried to stuff you with your pillow."

Felix cut me off. "Rick Martínez? What the hell?"

I described the visit to my office in the most paranoid terms I could articulate.

Felix stared out of the cabin's window into the twilight. He shook his head. "Martínez . . . after all these years. But

146

you're right, man. That guy had a grudge with roots in boot camp. He's liable to go off any minute. He was that way in Nam. He thought I didn't respect him and his *carnales,* almost as crazy as the gang stuff you're into now. You know, maybe I should call on that guy, even up something in my life."

"That's not what I'm saying. We can work this out—I know it. I don't understand it all, but Vietnam's a part, I guess. And Anglin. And, and . . ."

Felix finished my sentence in a way I hadn't anticipated, but it didn't surprise me. "And maybe Martha and Adela. I got twisted when I lost them, and now I couldn't survive if I lost another person I love."

Elizabeth stopped puttering with the pots and pans and slowly walked over to Felix. She rubbed the back of his shoulders.

I said, "Look, Felix. I feel like I'm in a movie. I've been watching everything happening around me, with you and Elizabeth, Victor. I don't have a connection with any of this, at least that I understand, but I've got to try something. Don't do anything until I get a chance to talk again with Harris. I'll arrange a meeting with him, do this right. We'll set up bail, get squared away with what Harris and the DA want to charge. Harris doesn't really want you. He wants to nail Anglin on something; he just hasn't figured it out yet. You can give him the reason."

Felix smiled. "You don't have to be involved. This is all my personal trip, my own bits and pieces of a demolished life that I'm trying to put back together. I understand, *vato,* and I thank you for what you've tried to do so far. I don't want any hassles for you, from Trini, the cops, nobody. I didn't kill anybody in Denver. But I could've easily if Anglin had tried to stop us. And that would've just brought heat down on you. Not good for anybody, man."

Elizabeth kissed him on the cheek.

Felix continued: "I won't have to do anything like that,

because Elizabeth's with me, and as long as that's true, I'm okay." The pot boiled over and water spilled onto the top of the hot stove, hissing and sputtering. Elizabeth rushed back to dinner and Felix and I opened two more beers.

The sounds that woke me faded away almost as soon as their existence had pierced my sleep-fogged brain. I stretched across the cot, trying to remember the layout of the cabin, trying to picture myself in the darkness of the upstairs loft, trying to imagine the cabin in the moonlight on the crest of the hill surrounded by the mountains and woods of the Valley.

Before I recovered my bearings, the sounds started up again. Immediately, I knew what they were and that they came from Elizabeth and Felix. In that epiphany of recognition and remembrance, I realized, without wanting to, that my friends no longer cared about staying quiet or not waking me or whether the cabin was on fire. For them, there was only the mutual point of ending that bore down on them like a runaway train.

There was nothing I could do to stop my intrusion into their privacy. I could not will myself back to sleep. I could not block out the sounds and I could not stop the image seductively parading through my skull—nude Elizabeth captured in a spell of passion and lust. Elizabeth's warm dark skin. Gentle, urgent hands caressing and reaching. Lips in familiar exploration.

The groans increased in tempo and then were replaced briefly by mumbled words. Flat on my back, with my eyes fixed on the window, I struggled to concentrate on the moon's halo. Unrelenting desire replaced embarrassment.

"Felix, Felix! Look in my eyes, baby. Uh-h-h."

Air entered and escaped her lungs in rapid, hard gusts. Felix whispered something. For several minutes, their thrashing, pushing, and mingling blocked out the dark-

148

ness and I saw with the clarity of a man watching minute life-forms through a microscope. I squirmed, changed positions, and toyed with the idea of thinking about my law practice.

And then Elizabeth finished, her love for Felix reduced to its essence.

"Oh, oh! I'm going to come. I love you. O-o-oh! Felix. I love you."

Felix gasped out his own expression of love. They laughed softly and then the sounds changed to those of a man and woman arranging themselves for sleep.

Elizabeth said, "I don't know what you do, but I love it, and I love you, Felix—more than anyone or anything I've ever known."

Felix's voice was muffled, as if he was talking into the pillow or, more likely, her hair as he snuggled against her in the bed. "*Querida*. With you, I'm young again. Hell, I feel like a man again, finally. Whatever it is between us, we work off of each other. Pretty good, no?" She murmured something I couldn't hear. "There is nothing I wouldn't do for you, Elizabeth. Not a damn thing. I'll kill Anglin if I have to." That was the Felix I knew, and his statement was surprising only because it was the first time I had heard him say it since he had let me in on the latest chapter of his love life.

Elizabeth spoke quickly. "Don't, don't. Don't even say anything like that. We'll work it out, baby. Don't worry anymore. Go to sleep."

"Think we woke up Louie?" They laughed again and then they were quiet.

My breathing felt heavy and forced. I imagined that they heard me and knew I had been their witness.

A collage of faces skipped across the moon—Dolores, Gloria, Teresa, Sylvia, and, finally, unexpectedly, Evangelina, and I wondered just what bizarre trip was coming down on me now.

17

When I left Felix and Elizabeth, I didn't feel good about it. I urged, begged, cursed, and threw legalese at them, but they were adamant in their decision. They didn't have definite plans. The most Felix promised was to keep me informed. I insisted that I would keep working in Denver on whatever I could to clear Felix's name. They accepted that, but it was clear that my concern over the possibility of Felix's arrest was not a priority.

During the drive back to Michael's house, with the rag-top in place, Felix quietly spoke about his past and future, describing disconnected particulars without urgency or panic. He talked about Elizabeth, the years on the streets when he had no identity, no name, and the series of terrible events that had sent him into his five-year vortex of agony and depression.

He convinced me that he was a haunted man, and a man treated as unfairly as any I knew.

Martha had been an English instructor at Community College and Felix was one of her students. He had returned from the war and decided to experiment with a few college courses. He dabbled with poetry and short stories and she encouraged him, but he gave up on writing. She, however, didn't give up on him. Talmage went nuts; he stormed into a police station and accused Felix of raping his daughter. That didn't go anywhere; the cops wrote him off as a nutcase. He didn't have any money then. He was just another bitter white man trying to sell real estate, blaming all his troubles on "the coloreds, Mexicans, and Commies."

He stayed out of their lives for years. Then the Denver boom in the seventies sent him over the top. He raked in money with a variety of schemes—computers, cable TV, more real estate. Felix described how, after years of not seeing the guy and then only after Adela was born, Talmage showed up to tempt Martha. He would dangle his new wealth in front of her, rail at her to dump Felix so that he could take care of Adela. The family went on without the father-in-law, of course.

"I think Talmage really was devoted to Adela. For a while, I put up with him for her sake. But he was too much. He'd come by and take her out for a ride, and by the end of the day, he had her so uptight and hyper that she couldn't sleep. When I laid down the law about what he could and could not do with our daughter, we had a raging argument and he cut us off completely. But he still sent cards to Adela, and always presents for her birthday, Christmas. I never shook my guilt about that. He was her grandfather! I just couldn't let her become influenced by his greed and hatred. She was so sweet, Louie. Too sweet for Talmage's way of life." The words were heavy and slow, difficult to say.

"I only saw her a few times, Felix. But I remember that she was a beautiful child."

"We had her for eight years. They were the best of my life."

Talking about the accident might help him, I thought.

151

"I never heard the real story about how she died. It was at a new house, or . . ."

"Adela tagged along with us that day. No school for some reason. Never quite remembered why. Martha had found a condo near the Capitol Hill area that she wanted us to move into. Condominiums were big then. Some developer had converted an old apartment complex. I didn't think it was right, not the kind of house for a kid. I wanted a real home, with a yard, a neighborhood. But Martha loved the view of the Botanic Gardens and Cheesman Park. I humored her and told her I would look it over."

He paused to maneuver the Impala across a cattle grate in the middle of the road.

"I wanted to inspect the place before I tried to convince Martha that it wouldn't do. It ended up being a family outing. Martha canceled one of her classes and packed a lunch for the park. The manager gave us a key and told us to look around at our leisure. Martha had good taste. It was a nice joint. Landscaping, maintenance, laundry— everything was taken care of. Each unit had its own entrance, with its personal elevator that took you straight up from the front door into the living room. Private access for the residents."

He drove without moving his eyes. I didn't see him blink or turn his head. He told the story as if it had just happened. I doubted that he would have seen anything on the road. He was seeing another day, different people, and he was somebody else, too.

"Martha and I were on the balcony, checking out her famous view, when we heard the rush of air, the sound of something dropping. That's all, man. No scream, no breaking cable, nothing. Adela had opened the elevator door and stepped in. Guess she just wanted to take a ride. Who knows? She fell the three floors and landed on top of the elevator car. Martha and I ran down the stairs and I struggled to reach her. But she was dead. Broke her neck."

I wanted to say something meaningful, something that would help him. "I'm sorry, man."

"That was it for Martha, of course. She blamed herself. It was her idea to move. She was the one who had found the condo and made us visit it. She asked herself why hadn't she kept her eye on Adela, thought of all the guilt trips she could come up with. Nothing I could do or say made her feel any better. I . . . . I didn't know what to do. I'm sure I added to her guilt."

He glanced at me and I saw that his pupils had lightened into a pale, watery ghost of the outrageous green that normally gleamed beneath his bushy brows, and his face had a horrible, frozen grimace. He sniffed and cleared his throat.

"The place was still empty six months later. Potential buyers must have been put off by the freak accident. And then one day I got a call from the police saying that Martha had somehow gotten in and jumped from the balcony. And that was it for me. I slipped into a crack between heaven and hell and vanished. I didn't see myself again for five years. Louie, I still dream about Adela, still watch myself lifting her from the elevator, my arms covered with blood, everything covered with blood. And Martha screaming in my ears, crying for hours."

I stared out the window of the car and the streaking landscape made me realize that Felix was doing at least ninety. I didn't say anything.

"You know, I made it through the war relatively okay, at least compared with some of the guys. I hadn't taken the time to figure it out. But I thought Vietnam had insulated me from a lot of things—the shock of death, good people suffering, life's basic bullshit. Whatever I had picked up in the war slipped away when I had to identify Martha's body." He slowed the car as Michael's place appeared over a ridge. "And there's no fucking way that I'm going to lose Elizabeth. I know you understand that, Louie."

What I understood was not the issue. But I played along with Felix. I had no choice, really. Elizabeth waited at the cabin for Felix so they could continue with their escape. Their foolish scheme bothered me, but I faced up to the fact that I could do nothing about it. I decided to focus my attention on Victor and Jenny, my other clients, and the rest of my life as Luis Montez, Ace Attorney.

I left Michael's house shortly after Inez drove into the yard and the kids roared into the house, back from Grandma's house. Michael's children were eager to tell their father about the strange sights and people of Pueblo.

While I hugged the kids and Inez, Michael and Victor had sealed their truce with a farewell handshake that appeared a bit forced. I was grateful for the symbolic meaning of the gesture.

Michael wished us well. "You guys come back, when you got more time."

Victor was as quiet as ever, but I believed—hoped—that his edge had been dulled a bit by the few days and nights away from the streets.

It seemed time to move on. I thought my role in the madcap adventure of Felix the Cat was finished. Okay—so once in a while my hunches are wrong.

Evangelina announced that Jenny was waiting for me to walk her over to the deposition. Two days after Victor and I had driven back from the Valley, Jenny was cooperating with me on the case that might help change the direction of her son's life. We had spent the previous evening going over her testimony and she still was solid. Her attitude had improved and I gave myself a little credit for that.

"I owe you for Victor—getting him out of the city until things cooled down with the Bloods, appearing for him in juvenile court."

"If you're worried about my fee, don't. It's part of—"

She interrupted. "No, I don't mean that. You've tried

with us, Louie. I appreciate it, and so does Victor, even though he might not ever tell you. The least we can do is stand with you in our own case against the cops."

I had prepared as much as I could in the short time since my return. I was confident, though, especially since I wouldn't have to do anything very complicated except sit at my client's side and give the city attorney and the police department's hired guns snide smiles each time she made a point for our side. I practiced my best look of righteous indignation.

Jenny talked nonstop from my office to the conference room in the city attorney's office, but I was not responsive. She didn't notice, or at least she didn't say anything about it. She was antsy about the deposition and my aloofness must have come off as typical lawyer psyche.

I didn't snap out of my lingering thoughts about Felix and Elizabeth until the deposition started and the first questions were fired at Jenny by Gary Yarbrough, whose job was to lay the groundwork for the defense in civil-rights and personal-injury cases filed against the city by aggrieved citizens. Waiting in the wings, sitting to the left of Yarbrough as a spectator only, was Kyle Radison, specialist in representing police officers accused of overstepping the bounds placed on them by various city and state laws and by a couple of paragraphs in amendments to the Constitution. Kyle was the guy the city brought in when the chances were good that a case would actually go to trial. He had apparently been very busy. His clothes were rumpled and an industrial-strength cowlick jutted from the back of his thinning hair. I considered suggesting a cup of coffee and a comb.

Radison barely acknowledged my existence. He stared at his legal pad and wrote detailed notes as Yarbrough went through the questioning. He had walked in the conference room with only the pad in his hands; he had to borrow a pen from Yarbrough.

There are trial attorneys, and there are litigators. Plenty of lawyers prepare for settlement without the slightest intention of ever setting foot in a courtroom. These litigators become quite adept at taking depositions, shooting off page after page of interrogatories, filing pretrial motions, and engaging in hours of expensive negotiations until finally an agreement is made that ensures all the legal expenses are taken care of, and, oh yeah, a little bit for the client, too. Sometimes the insurance company pays, sometimes the taxpayers cover the bill, and sometimes the victim barely escapes without additional injury.

Radison was a trial attorney. He prepared his cases for the courtroom, not a settlement conference. Opponents more often than not worked something out with him because it was painfully obvious that while they were still putzing around with their third set of interrogatories, he was finishing up his opening statement for the jury. He was the kind of lawyer who made me work a little bit harder. He provided the challenge I needed so that I could relish sticking it to him in front of a jury. In anticipation of the battle, I had outlined my closing argument for Jenny's case about a week after she had retained me to help her, and I knew that she had a winner.

I wanted the chance to tangle with Radison. But with Yarbrough in charge of the initial skirmishes, the odds of appearing soon in a courtroom on Jenny's behalf were close to nonexistent. Yarbrough litigated—and delayed.

Yarbrough plodded through question after question about Jenny's education, medical history, her family, her criminal record, her son's record, her well-documented—and successful—struggle with drug addiction, the history of her ex-husbands and current lovers, her penchant for rabble-rousing, and, finally, ugly—and unfounded—allegations about child abuse. She almost lost it a couple of times, but I managed to rein her in by making timely objections to Yarbrough's questions.

156

Three hours into the deposition, Yarbrough asked his first question about the night she was beaten.

"You had been drinking that night, right?"

"Of course. I was in a bar. I had two beers and one shot of tequila. I was with a girlfriend. It was her birthday."

"How intoxicated were you?"

She grinned and played along. "I wasn't intoxicated. It wasn't my party. I stayed straight. I was supposed to drive everybody else home. I never got the chance to do that. I was mauled and knocked around by Marsh and Thomas and ended up in jail."

"We'll get to that, Ms. Rodríguez. Try to stick to answering just my questions."

Jenny rolled her eyes.

The questioning continued. Occasionally, I made an objection, more for appearance's sake than anything else. I relieved my boredom by interjecting a comment here and there, but it was clear that on that day Jenny didn't need a lawyer.

She had her story and was sticking to it. Yarbrough couldn't get much out of her except for the straightforward facts—she had been paraded to the bar's parking lot after the raid. She'd basically stood around, watching over her inebriated friends, when Thomas and Marsh singled her out and began to degrade her in front of the crowd. Apparently, the two cops were aware of her minor celebrity status and the scene provided a good opportunity for them to upgrade their image and improve community and police relations.

"I know Thomas and Marsh. They've terrorized the Northside for years. They like to stop cruising Chicanitos and scare the hell out of them. I've confronted them before about their gestapo tactics and they haven't liked it. To tell you the truth, I wasn't that surprised when Thomas let me have it with his baton and Marsh turned that dog loose on me."

"You weren't surprised?"

"Not really. When you grow up where I did, in the pro-jects, you learn that there are some okay cops and there are some real animals, guys who get their kicks by beating up kids, harassing innocent people, and solving petty drug-possession cases by intimidating drunks, junkies, and other losers. Marsh and Thomas fit into the animal category."

"You don't like the officers, do you? You have no respect for their authority or position."

The question was a setup. Whatever Jenny answered, it wouldn't look good in stark black and white on a tran-script page. But I had a certain amount of respect for my client and so I let her respond without throwing out any stalling tactic.

"Am I supposed to respect the assholes who broke my wrist, bruised my kidney, and gassed my lungs? Would you respect that, Mr. Yarbrough? Because if you would, then I want you to go out with me this weekend and you can get a taste for yourself. We'll see what you respect and what you don't."

Radison looked up from his pad, straight into my eyes. That's when I sensed Yarbrough would call in the next few days with an offer. Radison would never get involved with the settlement talks, but, based on his word, the city would fold. The experienced trial attorney had seen the tough-ness in Jenny, felt her indignation and pride. He might be willing to chance it and try to rattle her in the courtroom, but he also knew that Marsh and Thomas were sorry examples of police officers who had histories exactly as Jenny had described them. Maybe he calculated the odds on selling a jury on yet another lawsuit in defense of cops who crossed their famous thin blue line and beat out their frustrations and anger on the public they were supposed to serve and protect. And maybe we just caught him on a bad hair day.

*   *   *

Felix made it sound easy. "Meet us in Española, guy. The festival is a good time. We're tired of hiding out. We'll dance and get drunk and party, and then we're gone. One last *borrachera* and Elizabeth and I split. We want you there."

"Too risky, Felix. Out in the open like that. You'll be sitting ducks." I frowned at the phone.

"We'll probably be safer in a crowd than driving around these spooky dirt roads. Come on, man. *¿Qué dices?*"

Evangelina helped me with the details of flying out for the weekend. The plan was for Felix to contact me at Evangelo's bar in Santa Fe. It was crazy. I have no excuse. But that's the way it was that year.

18

*H*ow had I let Felix talk me into this?

I didn't have time to come up with an answer. Thick, rough hands grabbed my collar and lifted me from the dirt. For a second, I wiggled for freedom, suspended in midair, but the grip of a powerful man secured me and I anticipated pain before he released me. Unexpectedly, he set me down on my feet and casually patted away the dust on my shirt.

"*Q-vo, loco.* You're lucky I found you, lucky I recognized you. You could be stretched out *a campo raso*, man, dead."

It took a heartbeat or two before I connected the face with a memory. Juan Salazar loomed larger than I remembered from the county jail of my youthful crime wave. He was older, naturally, with a shock of solid gray hair under his cowboy hat, but ever ponderous, and threatening.

"What the hell is going on, Juan? What is this?"

"*¿Qué* strange, eh? Last time I saw you, I was on my way to the Colorado *pinta* for that number with the Lunas, more than twenty years ago. Did my time. *Gracias a Dios*, it wasn't a life sentence. Came back home, got a job with my cousin, Tony C. Only work I could get. Guy's *familia* owed mine. Same old thing, you know how it is."

"But what are you doing out here . . . in this? Back at the dance . . . And Felix and Elizabeth, what about them?" The crash caught up with me and I lost my balance from wooziness. My neck and back muscles tightened into a stiff sheet of rusty iron. Based on the size of my headache, I calculated that a piece of bumper must have sliced my head in two. Juan helped me to a flat moss-covered stone. I gingerly sat down.

"Easy, *vato*. You might have cracked something. You were thrown from the car. Been out for almost a half hour. You're lucky to be alive."

Ol' Lucky Luis Montez, that's me. I took a deep breath and waited for him to explain.

"I knew who you were right away. I remember guys I did time with, and you, man, always reading, trying to stay out of everybody's way. You were okay with me. I knew you were into a bad scene when I saw Ernesto López at your side. *¡Un cabrón loco! Y, pos,* he ran a game on me not long ago. Paybacks, *ése.* We wrestled around for a few minutes at the dance, *pero* he got away from me just as the cops showed up. I knew Tony had been hit, but there wasn't anything I could do about that. I could do something about López. For my cousin, I went after him. I jumped in the band's *troca* and followed him out here. Good thing, too. You guys were tearing ass. *¡A la madre!* When you flew off the road, López and his pals kept on going. They'll probably circle back." He saw me looking around for signs of Elizabeth or Felix. "They took off, man. It's just you and me, *ése.*"

That caused a little anxiety. My memories of Juan were the dark, on-the-edge-of-violence images I carried from my short stay in the county jail. He had finished the young lives of two brothers in an ugly barroom brawl, then played the role of the unquestioned macho boss in the jail. Standing before me in the cool New Mexican night, in a Tony C. promotional T-shirt that barely concealed his web

161

of tattoos and snug jeans that displayed the fact that he still carried excess weight, he retained the look of a man who could snap me in two with the flick of a wrist.

"Thanks for the help, Juan. I'd explain, but it's a long story. You look good, man. It has been a hell of a long time."

"Felix and Elizabeth told me what's going on. *Simón*, bud, it has been a long time." He grinned and wrapped his arms around me in a bear hug that soon had me gasping for air. Whatever lump of hatred Juan had carried with him had softened. Not that he had changed completely. He was obviously still a strong man, and a man who skipped along the brink as he traveled from one gig to another with his cousin's band. And I wouldn't want to meet him head-on in any kind of challenge. But the grin, the hug, the shine in the eyes told me that he had gathered and put aside some warmth from somewhere along the way. And now he had befriended me two decades after our brief crossing of paths when he was the wild young killer who loved music and I was the screwed-up kid accidentally digging out bits of misplaced cultural identity wherever I could find them, including a county jail.

He explained our immediate problem. "We have to get back, man, check on Tony. It looked bad. And López's men are going to find us *en un ratito.*" As an afterthought, he added, "Your friend left this for you."

He handed me a message scribbled on the back page of the program from the festival. I made out the words the best I could with the help of the moon and stars.

> Louie—Got to make this quick.
> Anglin's men might return any sec.
> Chato saved our asses. We borrowed
> the band's van. Report it to
> the cops as stolen. We'll leave
> it the first safe place where

we can get another ride.
I said you'd help out if your
old pal got hassled about
losing the van. We're long gone.
You're safer without us around.
Hope you are all right.
You should be able to catch
a ride if the cops don't show up.
If Anglin leans on you about us,
Elizabeth says you should use
the files she left at the cabin.
She said you'd know what to do
with them. This is it, amigo.
We ain't coming back.
Gato.

I stuck the note in my shirt pocket and was about to ask
Juan for directions to the quickest way back to the highway so that we could try to hitch a ride. Ernesto's voice cut
through the night and stopped me.

"Put your fucking hands over your head!"

He walked into the moonlight and I could see that he
held a gun. Juan jerked around to face him. Another man
stood next to Ernesto, but in the dark I couldn't tell
whether he also had a gun.

Juan moved toward Ernesto. Ernesto barked out an
order.

"Stop, Salazar! I don't know your link to *este vato*, but
stay out of this and you might make it back to Española."
He looked at me. "Where are your friends, Montez? My
guys are out there and we'll find them. But you know
where they're headed. Save us all some time. I'll get out of
here and you and this fat pig can start looking for a way
back to town."

"You're a lot stupider than you look if you think I'm
telling you anything about Felix." Juan laughed at my

brash words, but he was cut off when Ernesto jabbed him with the gun.

Juan roared at López. *"No tengo miedo,* López. I know the chickenshit you are." He dived at López's feet and knocked him to the ground.

"Fuck you!" The gun went off and I involuntarily jumped a few inches in the air.

I looked at the second man, who didn't seem to know what to do. I rushed him. To no one specific, I whispered, "No gun. No gun."

I tackled the man. He was sturdy and solid and my hands slipped off his waist. I punched for all I was worth and we both fell to the ground, where we rolled around slugging one another next to the grunting and kicking bodies of Juan and Ernesto.

I hadn't shaken the nausea from my recent bout with unconsciousness and the pit of my stomach told me I couldn't keep twisting, punching, and wrestling in the dirt. I reached for a rock and swung it in the direction of the man's head. It glanced off his nose—not a solid hit, but the impact caused him to turn me loose. Blood seeped from the cut and dazedly he tried to wipe it off his face. He hollered, "Son of a bitch!"

I lay on the ground, straining to keep from throwing up.

Juan danced around a crouching Ernesto. The knife in Ernesto's hand sliced and curled through the darkness. The gun lay about a dozen feet from the men.

Juan taunted López. He was bent over, one hand clutching the flesh of his rib cage, but his steady voice carried echoes from the county jail.

"Come on, *pinche.* Come and get it, if you got the balls. Use that *filero.* I'm right here, motherfucker. Come and get it."

Ernesto shrieked like a hyena attacking a piece of warm meat. He lunged and slashed Juan across the stomach. A wide dark stain spread across Juan's shirt. Juan grunted but didn't fall. He moved to his side and caught López around the neck as López's momentum carried him past his target. Juan wrapped his forearms around López's neck. He squeezed his plump vise. Ernesto's eyes swelled with terror. Juan cut off his air and broke his windpipe at the same time. He yanked the knife from López and jabbed it into López's shoulder. López kicked madly at earth and sky, but Juan held on until the spasms stopped. Juan fell back into the dirt. López lay at his side, neither man moving.

I jumped to my feet and picked up the gun López had lost in the struggle. I started after the man I had sideswiped. He knew that López was gone and that I had the gun. He turned to run, then stopped, apparently afraid that I might shoot him in the back. I was having trouble staying on my feet. I knelt on one knee and pointed the gun at him, but he weighed the risks and took off running. I couldn't see where he went. I pulled off a shot in the direction I thought he had taken. From my right, a gurgling sound was all I heard from Juan. López stretched across the earth, as still as the silent mountains that surrounded us. That's when I finally vomited.

Juan didn't make it. He had taken a bullet in the side from López's gun. That injury, combined with the knife wound, drained enough blood that he was gone long before any cops or ambulances showed up.

I think it was a bad night, even for New Mexico. Tony C. had been shot in front of several hundred screaming fans and his condition was described as critical on the TV news shows. If he died, an armed invasion of Española by his Texas fans and family wasn't too far-fetched. No one grieved over López's death. He was well known to the state troopers and county sheriffs who prowled the scene of his last knife fight. They joked obscenely and frequently about the ugly way he had cashed in. Juan was a mystery to the cops, but eventually his record would reveal his identity and the cops would breathe yet another sigh of relief. One less Chicano hard case.

All of which, of course, made me initially appear to be rather interesting to the New Mexican authorities. I did my best to keep them out of Felix's business. I said I didn't know any of the dead men, that one had picked a fight with me and then chased me from the dance, for no apparent reason, and that the other guy had helped me out. I played dumb—easy for me. I was knocked unconscious in the crash and when I came to, the dead guys were already dead. I just wanted to get back to Colorado and the safe confines of the Mile High City. It helped when my profession as a lawyer was confirmed. It also didn't do me any harm that the cops took it for granted that López didn't necessarily need a reason to start any *pedo,* chase me through the countryside, and end up stabbing and getting stabbed by a man the newspapers eventually called "the notorious Juan 'Chato' Salazar."

The names Felix and Elizabeth never entered the interrogation.

A premature beginning of summer rolled into the city and restored energy to the lethargic populace, including yours truly. I felt good back home, ready to get down to business. I worked the kinks out of my neck and tried to do the same for the kinks in my business. For a couple of weeks, I was able to do what I had to do to continue with my life as lawyer and my not easily shed role as the least eligible Denver bachelor. I picked up new clients, had a couple of dinners with friends of Evangelina, and avoided places where Trini Anglin might show up.

There was only one problem. A sparse story in the Regional section of the newspaper provided minimal facts about a fairly new van that had been found in the sand near the New Mexican town of Columbus, very close to the

Mexican border. It was burned out, gutted, and half-buried in a weedy ravine. Patches of blood and pieces of clothing were all the state police had found.

I retrieved Tony C.'s business card from my Rolodex and gave him a call. He was back in Texas recuperating from the Española show. The dramatic ending to his concert and the famous photograph of him bleeding and kneeling on the stage, clutching his bloodstained instrument, had made the national news and secured forever his place in the Chicano Hall of Fame of Crazy Things That Happen to Idols, Sex Symbols, and Heroes.

We had met at Juan's funeral, where I trusted him with most of the truth about the night Juan was killed so that he would know Juan hadn't reverted to his old ways. I didn't want Tony to think Juan had been involved with López.

Tony sounded pleased to hear from me and I took it for granted that he didn't mind talking, since I was at least partly responsible for the wave of publicity. I had played a minor role in the growing legend of Tony C. Maybe one day it would mean free tickets to a concert.

He told me over the long-distance line that the stolen van was totaled and the police assumed the passengers had been killed, probably by another set of bandits or as the result of bad blood among the original crew of thieves. Crooks killing crooks is a satisfying theory for most cops

The van had been pushed into the ravine, where it sat for a week before a Boy Scout troop on a camping trip unknowingly pitched their tents near it. According to Tony, the police expected to find a body or two buried somewhere close to the ravine. It definitely was not an accident.

So that was it. Felix and Elizabeth were more than likely dead—victims of Anglin's far-reaching scheme. The guy who had made it off the streets, through the war, through the hell of the death of his wife and child—his luck had run out and he had played his last hand, for love.

I acted out of instinct, as if I were a kid with Gato as we slowly made our way out of whatever jam we had fallen into, back-to-back, talking loudly and laughing nervously, two guys who didn't know any better but who somehow always managed to land on our feet. There was something I had to do for Felix.

19

When I heard the click of Tony's phone, I called Harris. He was out, but I left a message that I had to see him. He showed up about an hour later.

Harris made it easy for me. He came to my office and waited until I finished with a client. He didn't yank me into the station, didn't try to intimidate Evangelina. We knew what we had to talk about and I appreciated his professional attitude about the whole thing.

"Cut the crap, Montez! I should arrest you for harboring a fugitive. I'd bet my badge that you were with Grr-ara and Anglin's wife." Harris insisted on calling Elizabeth "Anglin's wife." "Cooperate and it goes easier on everybody, including me. I'm getting tired of this case. To tell you the truth, I'm happy that Cuginello finally got his. But I have to wrap it up. Your buddy is the guy. His service records confirmed that he was a sharpshooter in the marines. The shots that nailed Joey Cugie were well within his ability. Whether it was done to get rid of the competition for Anglin's wife, I don't know. Doesn't really matter, as far as I'm concerned. Give me the information I need and I'll get on with it. Don't make it worse for yourself."

"Who do you want, Harris? Felix or Anglin?" I picked up a file of papers from my desk. I thumbed the pages so that Harris could see the ledgers, statements of accounts, copies of letters and handwritten notes.

"What are you trying to pull now? If you've got evidence that's relevant to the investigation, turn it over and quit screwing around. You know the rules as well as I do. You should follow them better."

"Be nice, Harris. I'm not sure what I've got here, so I can't be accused of withholding evidence. In fact, I intended to turn this over to you today. It was, uh, delivered anonymously. Probably an acquaintance of Anglin's who heard I've got a grudge against the guy because of Felix. Looks like business papers and records and a few other items that might implicate Trini Anglin in a couple of schemes I'm sure you've been looking into. It seems to me that there is also enough in here to suggest that Anglin thought Cuginello was taking a bit off the top for himself from some of Anglin's dope rackets. I'm not a cop, but you think that might be a motive? You think maybe the old double cross might have some relevance to Cuginello getting blasted into Cherry Creek? Why don't you take a look, Harris, and tell me what you think. And after you've finished, maybe you can tell me what you know about an outfit called Tri-Age Management?"

Harris pressed his fingers against his temples and rifled his blond hair. He looked pale and bleached-out against the earth tones in my office. But his eyes gleamed and his smile opened wide as he reached for the file. I thought Elizabeth would have appreciated the moment.

I jumped to a few conclusions. Even if they were wrong, they made me feel better.

Harris and I talked for a few more minutes and he left to do what he could with Anglin. I called it quits for the day and drove in the general direction of my house. Is it just me, or what? The tortured old brain cells roused themselves from their slumber and rushed around like kids at a birthday party, the creaky wheels started turning, and I went off on a fantasy about making things right for Felix and dragging down the bad guys in the process.

Before I fully appreciated what I was doing, I maneuvered the tank into the parking lot of a convenience store. I sat listening to the jazz station until a group of mean-looking children finished with one of the phones. I had the number for Tri-Age Management and with a little luck I thought I could get through to Talmage.

I got as far as the aide, Johnny. Yes, he knew who I was. What the fuck did I want? No, I couldn't talk with Talmage. What's the message?

"Tell your boss he should see me in about a half hour. Inspiration Point. Sheridan and Forty-ninth."

"You must be joking, Montez. Talmage isn't going to waste time on you, especially in some goddamn park. Get a life."

"Pay attention, cowboy. Tell him I want to talk to him about a guy they call the Cat. And Adela. Make sure you mention Adela."

My next call went directly to the party I wanted. He laughed in my face, but I had no doubt I would see him later.

There was one more detail I had to arrange. I didn't have as much luck with this one. I had to leave a message with an answering machine that cut me off before I was completely finished. By then, a sullen-looking gaggle of girls watched me and I concluded that I had made enough calls from their phone for one night.

I waited in my car at the top of the hill with the uninspired name of Inspiration Point. A make-out mecca and a good place to watch the city at night, the Point had been renovated since I was a kid with boiling hormones. Trees, shrubs, benches, and a waist-high wall added to the place's charm. A sidewalk wound west through the trees and along the wall to the end of the park where the view encompassed the western half of the city and the mountains. The wall circled back in an elongated oval. The amusement park was immediately south, and the Chipmunk and roller coaster rattled just beyond I-70. Denver's skyline towered in the background, off to the south and east. The interstate streaked into the mountains. Comfortable houses bordered the hill to the north, at the foot of the steep incline that dropped dramatically to the street.

In those few minutes, I summed up what Felix had meant to me. Crazy, out of control, belligerent, and defiant—that was Gato. Cool, smooth, and trustworthy—that was Gato, too. He had acted all his life from a core of values that included loyalty, pride, and bullheadedness. Somewhere along the line, he had dragged me along for part of his ride; I wasn't always sure it had been good for me. But, hey, there I was, in the dark, playing a hunch, waiting for two powerful men who could have me chopped up into little bits of Mexican hamburger, all because there was something I owed Gato and there was still a bit of his story to unravel.

The knock on the window jerked me out of my reverie. I stared into the barrel of Anglin's gun as he motioned me outside the car. He stood near Talmage and I could hear the hum of the electric motor that powered the wheelchair.

I guessed that Johnny had been left at the office when Anglin picked up Talmage. Anglin and Talmage must have reckoned on handling me by themselves, with as few observers as possible. Anglin's white Caddy had been parked unseen by me at the far corner of the lot.

Anglin spoke. "What a fucking moron. I told you not to screw around with any of this. Just couldn't stay out of it, eh? I ought to fuck you up just out of principle, you know what I mean? Stupid greaseballs need to get knocked around for their own good." The guy must have forgotten that he was half greaseball himself. His laugh was out of place in the quiet of the park. My jaw still carried a memento from the last time I had had a talk with Trini Anglin.

"Is that how you handled Elizabeth?"

He actually smiled as he took a step toward me, gripping the gun as if it was a flyswatter and I were an insect on the wall of his bathroom.

Talmage barked, "Control yourself, Anglin! Let's get this over with and get the hell out of here." Anglin stopped and pointed the gun at me again. Talmage naturally assumed the role of senior partner in the business relationship he had with Trini Anglin.

"What do you want, Montez? What is it that you think you have on Anglin and me? This better be good."

"It's not what I've got, Talmage. It's what Detective Harris has. I gave him all the information Mrs. Anglin collected over the years on your business partner's schemes. The last I saw, he was on his way to the DA's office. I wouldn't be surprised if you are in some of those records. Elizabeth was meticulous and very complete. But I think Trini knows that."

Anglin's smile dropped into a snarl. His teeth showed the hatred he felt for his wife. "That bitch! I knew she would try something. Her and that punk Cuginello." He stopped before he said any more about his late associate's unlucky involvement in the messy turn Anglin's financial and personal lives had taken. He looked around for a clue as to what he should do. Whatever Elizabeth had known about his business had moved him, in a matter of a few seconds, close to apoplexy.

Talmage moved away from Trini and even in the darkness I could see the disgusted look on his face.

"I told you about her years ago. I knew she would get back at you. All because you were too damn cheap to have somebody else take care of the paperwork for the business. You used your own wife!" Talmage's loathing oozed out of his mouth and flowed over the neatly trimmed grass and landscaping of the park. "You were supposed to have gotten rid of her and her boyfriend, but you couldn't even do that right! She and Cuginello made you for a jerk."

Trini took the old man's abuse almost graciously. Whatever their relationship was based on, it wasn't mutual respect.

I spoke up, wanting to confirm what I had created out of a few days of memories in the Valley and a few years of history with Gato.

"That's when you sent your own man after Felix, wasn't it, Talmage? It was too much of a coincidence that López had been in Central City only days before he latched onto me in Santa Fe. He was up here talking to you, getting his assignment. And that had nothing to do with Elizabeth and Anglin. It was all between you and Felix." Talmage looked at me as if I was a raving lunatic, and, at that point, I was very close. "López was your instrument of revenge, your last chance at fixing up the horror of your daughter's and granddaughter's deaths. You must have thought it appropriate that you hired one Chicano to kill off another. We're all expendable, anyway, right?"

Talmage mercilessly twisted his one good hand around the control knob of his chair. Anglin stared at him, worrying that there were too many details he suddenly didn't know about his partner. Talmage's voice had turned into a high-pitched squeal.

"This is all your fault, Anglin. You gave that whore enough time to get her records to this two-bit mouthpiece, and now I've got to clean up the mess."

Elizabeth had passed the papers on to me only as an afterthought. It never had been her plan to eke out any vengeance against Trini. The records were supposed to be my insurance policy. It was easy to see that the real reason

174

he had chased after her and Felix was not because of a cuckold's humiliation. Elizabeth had made herself privy to some of Anglin's most vital business dealings. He had finally acceded to Talmage's demands and determined to get rid of her. Then along came Felix, and the race was on. Felix and Elizabeth ran because of love and Trini chased them because he was a crook protecting his ass. It wasn't quite Romeo and Juliet, but then, in the nineties, what could be?

Talmage spoke again. "Like I said, Montez, what do you want? The cops may have pieces of evidence that this dumbbell let them get their hands on, but they've still got to make a case. Get a conviction, you know, all that legal procedure bullshit that you guys are so good at, for the right price. And I really doubt that I have much to sweat from whatever that bimbo put together. So I don't get it, don't understand what there is for you."

"You could say I'm an incurable romantic, Talmage." His stare told me that I was not being taken seriously. "Okay, okay, I may also be an idiot, but I want to believe that there is fairness for decent people and that creeps like you get what you deserve. I gambled that you two would meet me out here, and you did. It's a calculated risk that I'm going to get out of this in one piece."

Trini moved toward me to demonstrate the errors in my calculations, but Talmage stopped him with a shove from his chair. He wanted to hear what I had to say.

I took my cue and started talking as I looked around the park. They had escorted me along the sidewalk to the far corner of the hill, near the landmark boulder that marked an important point in the history of Colorado. Anglin occasionally jabbed his gun in my ribs, and I had no plan for any escape.

Talmage stopped his chair near the boulder. I waited at the crest of the hill. There was no more wall. Dirt and ground rock replaced the park's grass. Some of the houses were now lighted and the sun had done a quick fade be-hind the Rocky Mountains. Shadows covered the park. I kicked at the loose gravel and weeds.

"You've been after Felix for a long time. He took your daughter, ruined her life. Then, at least the way you look at it, he took your granddaughter, too, didn't he?"

This time, Talmage moved toward me, and I figured that my talking was just about over. Anglin was anxious, up-tight about being out in the open with his crazy sidekick and a long-winded Chicano who seemed to know too much. He carelessly rubbed the gun against the side of his face.

I was trapped against the beginning of the drop of the hill, with Anglin's gun covering my every move. We were in darkness and shadows, in a deserted park that seemed emptier than I had ever remembered. I heard traffic from the interstate and Talmage's heavy breathing.

I turned on my best closing-argument mode. "Tri-Age Management owned that condo; you guys were converting that whole block. I finally saw the obvious—Tri-Age: *Tri*ni and Talm*age*. Imagine my chagrin when that hit me." Talmage and Anglin didn't smile with me. "Felix was sup-posed to inspect the place, look it over for Martha and Adela. It wasn't too hard for you to arrange the elevator so that your son-in-law troubles would be over. How hard could it be to rig an elevator, especially in a building that's not finished? Of course, you didn't know that Adela and Martha would tag along with Felix that day. You couldn't know that the curious little girl would play with the but-tons on the wall, step into the opening door, and fall where you had intended to find Felix."

The wheelchair noise increased as Talmage pushed buttons and yanked at the lever.

I finished my speech. "You killed your granddaughter and brought on your daughter's suicide. You thought Felix's blood would wash you clean."

I had nowhere to go and nothing more to say.

Anglin turned and stared at Talmage. His partner might have gone too far, even for the darling of the Northside rackets.

Talmage was beyond words. That smell of fear and hatred that had almost choked me in his house flooded over us. He raced at me with his chair, gasping sounds escaping his throat as he aimed his machine at me. He charged and I was frozen to the spot where I had planted my shoes. The weight of his rushing wheelchair and my grinding heels broke up the dirt beneath us. It felt as though the entire hill gave way. I could see the lights in the houses below as I jumped to escape the crumbling earth. I landed on my knees in a bush of yucca and cactus. My pants ripped and a cactus needle jabbed into my thigh.

Talmage lost control of his wheelchair as a chunk of the hill crashed downward and the ground finished collapsing. He wrestled with his machine, desperately trying to use his one good hand, but it was too late. Talmage stared at me in that final instant before he rolled down the hill. He was strapped in his chair, trapped as it careened and tumbled down the steep incline. The dull sound of his smashed skull on the street pavement ended the fall—and my interest in him. I turned to Anglin and his gun.

"Just you and me, Montez. Time to rock and roll, as they say."

I was getting very tired of guns and threats and wrestling matches in the dirt. I felt my age in my knees and my punctured thigh and I knew I would be a loser in the confrontation with Anglin.

Anglin sighted his gun in the general direction of the upper half of my body. I started to stammer another story, hoping to distract him, when shadows in the moonlight moved across the grass. I stopped yammering. Anglin, almost casually, turned to take stock of the intruders. Leather baseball caps reflected silver-and-black images of ghoulish, deadly boys of summer whose pictures would never appear in packs of baseball cards. Victor and a good part of the CRB stood next to Anglin, inches from the gun and his hate-filled face. The juvenile creatures of the night were suddenly a source of hope.

"What the . . ." He moved to aim the gun at the boys, but they were on him with speed and precision that would have been envied by an Olympic team of gymnasts. A flurry of punches and kicks dropped Trini to his knees. His grunting and groaning finally ended. That's when I stepped in and grabbed Victor. His boys were ready to pounce on me, but he stopped them. I might have waited too long to interrupt the beating, but, on the other hand, it was one of those times when I didn't have much trouble ignoring my whimpering conscience.

"Thanks, Victor."

" 'S cool, Louie. Lucky for you Jenny figured out your message and tracked me down. Felt good to get back a little justice for Petey. You want us to, uh, take this piece of shit . . ."

"No, Victor. I think you've done enough." They ambled back down the path, laughing and joking, just a bunch of kids out for fun and games in the city. I picked up Anglin's gun.

Someone from the houses called the cops and an ambulance, and, eventually, Harris found me holding the gun on the unconscious Anglin. He dragged Anglin away and ordered me to meet him downtown to make a statement.

I sagged against the red boulder. In the lights of the cop cars and ambulance, the plaque hanging on the boulder, faded to copperish green, delivered a succinct summary of the early history of the state and proudly proclaimed the driving motive for the westward expansion of civilization.

ONE MILE NORTH OF THIS POINT
GOLD WAS DISCOVERED
ON JUNE 22, 1850
BY A PARTY OF CALIFORNIA-BOUND
CHEROKEES. THE DISCOVERY WAS MADE
BY LOUIS RALSTON, WHOSE NAME
WAS GIVEN THE CREEK
(A BRANCH OF CLEAR CREEK).
REPORTS OF THE FIND
BROUGHT THE PROSPECTING PARTIES OF 1858,
WHOSE DISCOVERIES CAUSED THE
PIKE'S PEAK GOLD RUSH OF 1859,
WHICH RESULTED IN THE
PERMANENT SETTLEMENT OF COLORADO.

20

Evangelina tossed the file on my desk. "Here's Victor's paperwork. The hearing with Judge Burgett is next week."

There was a good chance that the proceedings involving Victor would be continued, and probably continued again. As long as Victor remembered his manners, Maggie Burgett would cut him some slack—provided, of course, that I retained my involvement with the Rodríguez family. The new case against Anglin had overshadowed the "major drug investigation" that Assistant District Attorney Taylor T. Giles had pompously paraded before the judge. But Victor was a long way from the straight and narrow. I owed him my best shot at giving him a chance.

"And Rick Martínez said that he appreciated your help with the VA benefits appeal, but he's traveling on—places to see, as he said. Kind of glad to see him go. Gave me the creeps."

"There go his checks. With him moving around, the VA will never catch up. Guy can't buy a break. And don't disparage the clients. I'd bet he's heading for Columbus, New Mexico."

She wrinkled her nose, then continued with her list of things for me to do.

"Willy Guzmán wants you to call. There's something else about your car. But you've got to wait until next week to reach him. He and his wife left on vacation."

"I can't fucking believe it."

"Now, now. Kind of touchy, aren't we?"

"Screw that. What else?"

"Detective Harris. Said he wants to set up a meeting with you and the DA for Anglin's preliminary hearing. Something about you being a star witness." I laughed and Evangelina shook her head. "You're crazy, Louie. You know that?"

"How long you been working for me?" She geared up for a smart-ass response, but I stopped her. "Don't answer. Just kidding, Evie."

She was about to walk out of the office. I said, "Can you get together whatever I've got on Felix and his business, house, all that? I guess I need to arrange his affairs, as the probate lawyers say."

"You okay with this thing about Felix? You want to talk about it? You guys were close."

The office was awash with sunshine from the wide, expansive bay window that looked out on Federal Boulevard. Evangelina and I had been busy with legal work, so my desk and conference table were cluttered with files, papers, notes, and letters. The place looked prosperous and bustling. The sadness was buried in the light and papers, unobtrusively lodged near the core of my heart, and I hoped that only Evangelina could sense it.

"There's not much to say. Can't really believe he's gone. You know, they never found any bodies. Anglin's sticking to his story that it was Talmage who hunted Felix. He says he had nothing to do with it and won't give any information."

"He wouldn't even if he did, that's for sure. He deserves whatever the courts throw at him, if anything."

There was some doubt. Trini had hired a high-profile defense lawyer, known for his flair, floppy hats, and success with juries. Anglin still might walk, especially if I was the "star witness." At times, my credibility was easy pickings.

The drug case against Anglin seemed strong, but the rest of it was shaky. The bribes, shoddy construction work, unhealthy connections to local politicians, extortion, and miscellaneous crimes against the public were complicated and difficult to trace back to Anglin. My testimony would help with some of the charges, but the key was in the records Elizabeth had conveniently made available. I doubted that they were admissible as evidence. Anglin's defense lawyer would have a field day tearing apart the reliability of anything based on an adulterous wife's motives.

I believed that Elizabeth had loved Felix. If it hadn't been for her too slick handling of Cuginello the night he shot up my house and the timing of Joey's death, I wouldn't have thought twice about her commitment to Gato. I had wanted the best for both of them, and I tried to minimize Harris's suspicions about her and Joey Cugie as just another crazy thing about that year.

"I sit here, understanding that Felix and Elizabeth are dead, that they never made it out of New Mexico, that they knew the price they might have to pay. And it's ironic that Talmage's money found a way to get to Felix after all this time had passed. I don't think Felix ever understood what was chasing him. I know all that, I understand it, and yet every time the phone rings, every time I see an envelope in my mailbox at the house, I think, Maybe Felix. They got away, they're on the beach in Mexico, drinking a shot of tequila to their old buddy Louie back in the States, and they've got the greatest thing going that two people could have. I can't help it, that's what I think. You're right, I am crazy."

The phone rang. I twitched in my seat and Evie gave me a funny, quizzical look. She laughed a bit nervously. She turned again to walk out. I picked up the phone, but before I said hello, I whispered something to Evie's back. She stopped and said, "What? What was that, Louie?"

I found my voice and repeated, "You doing anything tonight? Like to try a movie, dinner? Larry Olguín and Cariño Nuevo are playing at the Dark Knight Lounge." Then I turned to the phone.

MANUEL RAMOS is a lawyer and part-time professor who has written several crime fiction novels, stories, and essays. He lives with his wife, Flo, in Denver, Colorado, where he continues to contemplate the fate of Luis Montez. For more information, visit his Web site at www.manuelramos.com.

ALFREDO VÉA JR. is a wild and unrestrained soul that wakes each morning to find itself trapped in the body of a Mexican male who has somehow managed to become a criminal defense lawyer and a novelist (*Gods Go Begging, La maravilla, The Silver Cloud Café*). This Mexican male body lives in the San Francisco Bay area and is married to a beautiful Italian wife and he has two Italian cats internationally known as the Fratelli Brothers. With a lot of wine and music he manages to keep body and soul together.

ILAN STAVANS is the Lewis-Sebring Professor in Latin American and Latino Culture at Amherst College. His books include *The Essential Ilan Stavans* and the best-selling *Hispanic Condition* and *On Borrowed Words*. His work has been translated into half a dozen languages.

Latino Voices

General Editor
Ilan Stavans

Editorial Board
Francisco Goldman
Achy Obejas
Judith Ortiz-Cofer
Johnny Payne

LATINO
VOICES

Treasures in Heaven
Kathleen Alcalá

Zigzagger
Manuel Muñoz

The Ballad of Gato Guerrero
The Ballad of Rocky Ruiz
Blues for the Buffalo
The Last Client of Luis Montez
Manuel Ramos

The Nature of Truth
Sergio Troncoso